D1436666

VAL FORREST IN THE FIFTH

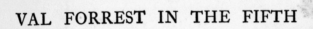

BLACKIE & SON LIMITED
50 Old Bailey, LONDON
17 Stanhope Street, GLASGOW

BLACKIE & SON (INDIA) LIMITED
Warwick House, Fort Street, BOMBAY

BLACKIE & SON (CANADA) LIMITED
TORONTO

VAL FORREST
IN THE FIFTH

BY

EVELYN SMITH

Author of " Binkie of III B ", " Nicky of the Lower Fourth ", &c.

Illustrated by J. Dewar Mills

BLACKIE & SON LIMITED
LONDON AND GLASGOW

Girls' School Stories

Catriona Carries On. Doris A. Pocock.

The Girls of the Rose Dormitory. Joy Francis.

The Greystone Girls. Joy Francis.

Biddy at Greystone. Joy Francis.

Terry's Best Term. Evelyn Smith.

Seven Sisters at Queen Anne's. Evelyn Smith.

Binkie of " III B ". Evelyn Smith.

Nicky of the Lower Fourth. Evelyn Smith.

The Little Betty Wilkinson. Evelyn Smith.

Septima at School. Evelyn Smith.

Phyllida in Form III. Evelyn Smith.

Miss Honor's Form. E. C. Matthews.

Lavender at the High School. E. C. Matthews.

The Latimer Scholarship. Olivia Fowell.

Hilda at School. Phillis Garrard.

Printed in Great Britain by Blackie & Son, Ltd., Glasgow

Contents

Illustrations

VAL FORREST IN THE FIFTH

CHAPTER I

The Viola Girl

The Fifth Form were talking.

" It's all green and gold outside," said Julie.

" I should like," said Corinna, " to be mounted on a wild mustang, careering over the pampas-covered plains."

The Fifth took this quite calmly, all except the two new girls, the one with the small head and short thick dark hair, whose name every one knew was Val, and the one with the blonde ringlets, whose name no one had heard. They looked a little surprised. For Corinna was wispy and pale, with eyes and hair that seemed as if they lacked strength to decide what colour they would like to be, and hands that never held anything quite hard enough, and a slight stoop.

" Life is hard," said a tall girl in the corner, with a beaky nose and a deep voice. " You can't hire a mustang in Dakin Priors, and all the pampas grass you'll ever see will be in the fire-place or the bamboo stand of the seaside lodgings."

" No mustang for me," said Julie. " I hate horses; they're such jerky creatures. A nice little two-seater on a tarmac road, and all the other cars in England safely garaged, and luncheon at the sort of hotel you read about, with lobster mayonnaise and strawberries and cream."

" I'm hungry," said a dismal voice from the back row.

" I'm *always* hungry," sighed Julie. " It alarms me a bit sometimes. I hope it doesn't mean that there's anything wrong."

" It does," said the beaky girl.

" *Does* it? What?"

" Greed," said the beaky girl.

" There's something unsympathetic about you, Pauline," complained Julie. " I've noticed it before."

" It would be glorious if food didn't count so much, though," said Pauline, in a conciliatory tone. She was just then trying to achieve stoicism, as the Fifth understood it. " Supposing you really didn't notice particularly *what* you were eating——"

" Glorious! I think it would be a piece of real bad luck!" said Julie. " Imagine not distinguishing be-

tween an éclair and a school bun. It would be worse
than bad luck, it would be low ignorance."

"Well, I'd like to be able to get on without things
I want," said Pauline.

"And I'd like to get all the things I want," said
Julie.

"Oh, I'd like some money!" cried the new Val.
"A pocket-book with a fat wad of notes, or a leather
bag of gold."

It was as if the wish had jumped out before she
noticed it, and when she heard her voice she flushed a
little, and looked down at her desk. She had spoken
so vehemently that the Fifth glanced at her curiously.
Not that it was odd to want money; so many jolly
things could be bought with it, but there was something strange in showing your desire quite so clearly,
almost as if you meant to hand round the hat immediately. Val felt that too, as soon as she had spoken.
It wasn't decent to own you wanted money so much—
it was like displaying a boil or a scar. What would the
others think of her? Not much. But if they only knew
—if they only knew half, they'd understand why the
wish had hopped out so quickly, before she could
control it.

As a matter of fact they did know a little. They had
heard of the failure of Marraby's Bank, because everyone had, and they had heard that the mother of Val
Forrest, the new girl whose name they had at once

found out, had lost most of her money and had gone to live with distant relations in Montreal, and that Val was boarding with a Mrs. Wilby, who had rented a partly furnished house which entertained them, because it was called The Turret and hadn't one. Those were the outstanding facts, and, as Val was still a stranger to them, they knew no others.

Miss Sylvester came in and the Fifth sat up and were politely silent. During the next few minutes Val learned that the ringletted girl was called Aileen. She stared at her moodily, noticing her new slippers, new attaché-case of the best hide, gold-nibbed fountain pen, platinum wrist watch with blue enamel face, perfectly tailored skirt, and blouse of rough silk, striped in the colours of Myra Dakin's girls' school. " How expensive she is!" she thought. " What will happen to me when my present coat and skirt wear out? Why *does* she do her hair in those corkscrew curls? Mother's pet, I suppose, or one of those Peter Pans—never means to grow up. I wish I were a pet. It seems ages since I was, and I don't suppose I ever shall be again."

" —and I'd like to hear the new girls' voices. Valentine, you might read Viola, and Aileen the Sea Captain, Scene 2."

Val quickly opened her *Twelfth Night*. The Fifth listened. They slid sidelong glances at the readers. They looked at one another. They looked at Miss

Sylvester to discover if they were permitted to laugh, and, deciding that they were not, began to endure, as well as they could, painful spasms of suppressed hilarity. It wasn't that Val and Aileen read badly. But Val's voice was a deep bell, and slight nervousness deepened it; while Aileen's was high-pitched, and extreme shyness sharpened it to a thin squeak.

"Change parts," said Miss Sylvester.

"Couldn't they do Sir Toby and Sir Andrew in the next scene?" suggested Pauline, who was a manager, and didn't like to see such good comic contrast running to waste.

Val looked a bit anxious, for she had not the power of the born actress to shift her personality, and she guessed that she could not interpret the humour of Sir Toby; Aileen, who had read the play before, thought it insulting to be suggested for the foolish Sir Andrew. She gave Pauline a glance which was evidently intended to put that character in her place for ever. Val, happening to see it, thought of a white rabbit trying to look like an eagle.

"Sir Andrew seems to be the sort of character I always get," said Corinna cheerfully.

"Well, I'm always the fool," said Julie. "Each man in his life plays many parts, but I always know in advance what Miss Sylvester'll give *me*."

"Do you?" said Miss Sylvester, as if struck by it. "Do I *really*? I don't believe it. But I'll be Feste the

fool myself, and you shall have a good romantic part
—Orsino, say."

" Oh no. I'd rather be the fool. Pauline can have
Orsino."

" I'm going to be Malvolio," said Pauline, with
imperturbable gloom. " Miss Sylvester gave me my
part first, as soon as she came in, without thinking
twice about it."

Miss Sylvester laughed a little.

" I'll be Malvolio," she offered. " You shall be the
hero if you like, Pauline."

Pauline shook her head.

" Malvolio for me," she said.

" Orsino seems to be going begging."

" We don't like him," said the Fifth.

" Well, who *will* be Orsino?"

" I'd like to," said Val, shyly.

Miss Sylvester considered her. There was something at once lost and gallant in the look of her that
suggested the heroine of *Twelfth Night*, cast on the
unknown island shore, and making the best of it.

" But you're rather good as Viola, you know," she
said. " If we can find a deeper voice for the man who
happens to be with you."

The Fifth laughed reminiscently. Aileen gave them
another hurt and stately glance. But Val was in it,
interested, more like herself than she had been since
the failure of Marraby's and the breaking up of home.

" But it says further on about Viola's voice—

Thy small pipe
Is as the maiden's organ, shrill and sound,"

objected Pauline. " You couldn't call Val's a small
pipe, could you?"

The Fifth were tickled at the very idea. Aileen
drew herself up, prepared for the delighted announce-
ment that *hers* was a genuine maiden's pipe. But it
did not come.

" Oh, comparatively," said Miss Sylvester. " We're
talking too much. Let's get on."

They got on. No one, except Aileen herself, seemed
to notice that one new girl had retreated to the back-
ground of the picture, while the other was being tried
for both hero and heroine of the piece. Val was too
much interested in what was going on to realize that
she had, for an hour at any rate, jumped from ob-
scurity. But it was in gayer spirits than usual of late
that, at the end of the morning, she went towards the
stuccoed villa residence that she now called home. She
often wondered what her mother would have thought
of it, had she seen it before sailing for Canada.

Through a highly varnished gate she passed into
a garden duller than one would believe a garden could
be. A broad gravel path was bordered by beds of
arid mould, planted at intervals with pansies which
did not seem capable of spreading, but just of keeping

up the size of the small tufts they were when first brought from Metcalfe the nurseryman. The plots of grass beyond the beds were neither shorn to velvet nor allowed to grow luxuriantly—they were cut just short enough to lop off the heads of the daisies. By the wall were a few herbaceous plants, curiously depressed in appearance, as if they simply could not summon up enough interest to grow. There had been a lily-bed, but it had been dug up during the war to make room for potatoes that steadily refused to flourish. In a corner was a rockery where a few of the commoner ferns just kept themselves alive among carefully cleaned stones. By the kitchen door was a bed of rhubarb. There were no weeds. Val thought that it would have been a relief to see dandelions, fool's parsley, thistles, anything growing in jolly flaunting profusion, as though it were enjoying itself.

Very carefully she wiped her feet on the door-mat marked SALVE, and then hesitated, trying to remember if she was supposed to ring the bell and wait, ring the bell and walk in, or simply walk in. The last seemed the most reasonable procedure, and she was nearly certain that she had just touched the electric button yesterday, and that it had been the wrong thing to do. But as she went quietly across the hall a door opened and Mrs. Wilby, with her usual air of remaining calm under great provocation, looked out.

" Oh, it *is* you," she said, with one hand pressed to

her throat. " Do give *some* indication when you come in, dear, will you?"

" I'm sorry," said Val, wondering, if ringing the bell were forbidden, what that indication might be.

" You creep about so *stealthily*," went on Mrs. Wilby, with an apologetic laugh, " that it makes one wonder who *has* come into the house."

Val hopelessly remembered that, a day or two ago, she had been reprimanded for thundering up and down stairs like a great hippopotamus. The elation of the morning dying down, she went up to her narrow little room, furnished with a small iron bedstead short of one foot, a chair of shiny yellow wood, a dressing-table that should have worn a white muslin petticoat and didn't, a corner fitment where her clothes hung behind what had once been a dining-room tablecloth of the old-fashioned kind, and her own suit-cases. It seemed to exult in its unfriendliness, in the impossibility that it would ever be hers.

" Talk about being cast ashore on a strange island," she thought to herself. " It would be nothing to this— nothing."

Luncheon was laid in what Mrs. Wilby called the morning-room, for no reason Val could imagine, except that it did not get the morning sun. As the garden was practically flowerless, this, and all the other rooms in the house, were without books, though Val still hoped to discover some. " They must be *some-*

where," she thought. " You couldn't live as many
years as Mrs. Wilby has done and escape being given
a book as a present, by someone who didn't know
you didn't want it, or having one left with you."
But it seemed as if you could, and Mrs. Wilby had
proved it.

The meal, like all at The Turret, was ceremonious
and unappetizing. Val's healthy schoolgirl appetite
tried to satisfy itself on a very small portion of hash,
and a dollop of watery blancmange, slightly burnt.
Ashdown, the one diminutive domestic assistant,
having lived on tinned salmon and sugar cake most of
her short life, knew nothing of cooking, and, as Mrs.
Wilby didn't believe in doing menial work or in in-
structing drudges to do it, it was quite unlikely that
she ever would. But Val was hungry enough to be
cheered by any kind or quantity of food, and her
spirits went up to the point of the morning.

" I'm going to like Myra Dakin's, I believe," she
said. " We had literature this morning, Shakespeare.
I read. Some of the time I was Viola."

" I suppose you *all* read, dear, as it was a reading
lesson. I can't say I care for *Henry IV*. Both dull and
coarse I thought it, a very poor play."

" But this was *Twelfth Night*. There's a lovely bit
at the beginning about music on a bank of violets,
only I can't remember the words."

" Then it's useless to speak of it, isn't it, dear?"

Val was silent, and, after a minute or two, Mrs. Wilby said quite affably:

" The Ellertons have asked me to take you over to Lyncote on Saturday, to meet Nina. They are thinking of sending her to Myra Dakin's, I believe, if they haven't yet done so. You will come across her there —though of course she will be in a lower form. She must be a younger girl than you are, such a pretty petite creature, such a joy to have in the home."

Mrs. Wilby's tone may not have been intended to make Val feel ugly, hulking, and a blight on home life, but it managed to convey this impression, and rather more. But Val was resolved to be agreeable. After all, her present guardian had been a friend of her mother's in former days at Myra Dakin's. She must be nice, if once set going in the right way. But she wasn't a self-starter.

" Oh, I'd like that," she said. Lyncote might be a friendly place, and Nina the sort of person who would make her feel gay and normal. She rather dreaded the thought of accompanying Mrs. Wilby on a visit, but she might be more cheerful in someone else's house than in her own.

" Make yourself presentable, dear, won't you?" went on Mrs. Wilby's gentle, pained voice. " See that your shoes are not down at heel and your gloves are good."

" Oh, my gloves and shoes are all right just now,"

said Val carelessly, wondering how long they would remain so, and what would happen when they were worn out. " It's tennis this afternoon," she added, as they got up from the table. " The girls play in gym dress, so I shan't have to get into white things."

" Tennis? There is a games' club, I suppose?"

" Yes."

" But, dear, won't that mean a subscription?"

Val flushed scarlet. She hadn't thought of it—of course, she wouldn't be able to play games. Bad as that was, she most disliked having been so foolish as not to have realized the necessity of the deprivation —to have been brought back to facts by Mrs. Wilby.

" Yes, it will. Idiotic of me," she muttered. " I'd forgotten."

" You mustn't be resentful, dear."

" I'm not."

" I don't like to see you flush up like that. Perhaps there's some little thing you can do here, to save Ashdown. Another person in the house makes a big difference, you know."

" Right. I'll save Ashdown," said Val, who was tickled by the appearance of the little maid, and sorry for her. " What's her Christian name?"

" Do these people have such things?" said Mrs. Wilby languidly. " I'm afraid I don't know, dear."

" I'll find out and tell you," said Val.

" Do. I'm glad you don't resent your position,

dear: I'm afraid you must undergo a few little dis-
appointments. But you must always remember that
you're a lucky girl—a very lucky girl, I think I may
say, in being able to attend Myra Dakin's."

"Oh, I will. I *am*." And, wondering what made
her so anxious not to let Mrs. Wilby know what she
really felt, Val rushed off to discover in what way she
might best " save Ashdown ".

CHAPTER II

Aileen, Val, and the Fifth

Pauline met Val at the form-room door when she came in next morning.

" Don't you play games?" she wanted to know.

" A bit—yes!" confessed Val, who at her previous school had played substitute centre-half in the hockey team and had won a trophy for swimming.

" You look that sort. Aren't you playing here?"

" I—I'd like to. Perhaps I could join later—at half term—when I've settled down a bit."

" The sub is five shillings," said Pauline. " That covers tennis balls." And suddenly she realized that this girl hadn't one shilling, let alone five. At once her organizing brain went to work. She liked the look of Val, her clean-cut boyish figure, the gallant way in which she held her little dark head, her grey eyes, with a sort of fear in them because of what had happened so quickly to her life, and courage, too, to meet it— the look that had made Miss Sylvester think of the wrecked Viola planning a way to meet her misfortunes. She wanted her to join the games club. Money was a nuisance—if Val were ill the form might subscribe to send her grapes and a bunch of roses, but it would be perfectly impossible to raise the games money for her while she was well. Something wrong there—perhaps some philosophy explained it.

"Can't you sell something you don't want?" she said abruptly. "An old stamp album, for instance. My young brother Thomas got tired of his collection. He didn't exactly sell it, now I come to think of it, he changed it for an owl under a glass shade, only *just* under, it's such a tight fit. Mother was greatly annoyed, for no one noticed the stamps, but the owl is a white elephant, or would be if it wasn't what it is, always in the way, and he won't keep it in his bedroom—I believe he's scared lest it should come alive in the night and make those terrible sounds they specialize in."

She hurried on, afraid lest the Viola girl should be offended. But Val took it quite calmly.

"You said yesterday, you remember, that you'd love to be able to do without things you want," she reminded Pauline.

"Yes, I know—but games, exercise, it's almost like one's bones. And it would be awfully nice if you joined."

After the constant fault-finding of Mrs. Wilby, the friendliness of the beaky girl was almost overwhelming. Val felt a sudden unexpected and dreadfully strong desire to shed tears. But she managed to laugh and say:

" If I bring in an owl under a shade to-morrow, you'll know I'm joining tennis. I'll do what I can, but I'm afraid it isn't likely."

" We'll hope for the best." And Pauline began industriously to check the accounts she had checked before, just to show what a perfectly matter-of-fact and ordinary conversation had just taken place. She stopped in the middle of a column as Aileen came in.

" Playing tennis?" she inquired.

Obviously Aileen resented the brusque business-like tone of the question.

" We have a court at home," she said, in her stately offended manner.

" Quite. Playing here?"

" No."

Pauline stroked through Aileen's name. So it appeared she didn't make a business of trying to persuade everybody. In her loneliness, Val found disproportionate pleasure in the fact that she was particularly wanted to join tennis. Only they couldn't be expected to go on wanting her if it were always impossible for her to do things. She must try to raise the money. Wild ideas thronged her brain—offering to supplant Ashdown, which wouldn't be fair, pawning her wrist-watch, which couldn't be done, winning a coupon competition, which wasn't likely. And Aileen could have paid the subscription twenty times over, and she just didn't want to join. " Not that I envy her," thought Val, with a glance at the resentful expression, and the childish, old-fashioned ringlets. " I don't. Not a bit."

If Val felt like that at the beginning of the morning, she was more certain of it at the end. There was, as usual, a crush in the senior cloakroom. The school buildings were old, dating back to the seventeenth century, and they had some of the inconveniences as well as all the beauties of their age. The room used as a cloakroom was far too small for the accommodation of the Fourth, Fifth, and Sixth, who complicated difficulties by wanting to put on their hats before the one small square of glass provided, an ambition which did not worry the juniors in the opposite room. The stand allotted to the Fifth was near this looking-glass, and the small space which they might call theirs was smaller by reason of the queue waiting, more or less patiently, hats in hands, for a brief contemplation and adjustment. The hat-pegs were too close together for comfort; there were no separate pigeon-holes for out-door shoes; the tap over the wash-basin dripped only one drop at a time: the conditions would have tried the best temper. And on this particular morning Aileen's temper was the one to suffer.

" Someone has hung her hat on my peg—number

twenty-two," she said, in the whining voice of the spoilt child.

" Don't worry too much. It's often done," said Julie.

" I thought Miss Dymchurch told us to be very careful to retain our own numbers."

" So she did, bless her. And we can retain the numbers all right—it's the pegs above them that are the problem."

" But where is my hat? This is not mine—*my* hat has disappeared."

" Don't know," said Pauline, making a slight movement to the left, as if that might be of some assistance.

" Please move, I have lost my hat," Aileen requested a tightly wedged quartette.

" Sorry—can't be done till my shoe is on," said Corinna.

" We can't move on till we move out," sighed Julie.

" Look—look—the glass is free!" A mad stampede followed, and Aileen, extremely mortified, retrieved a badly squashed straw hat trimmed with daisies from below the stand.

" It's ruined!" she declared tragically. " My hat is ruined."

" What was it like before the accident?" asked Julie.

" It's too bad!" She took the school sailor from its peg, glanced at the name inside, and flung it on the floor. " Valentine Forrest. She ought to know better, as she is a new girl too. One wouldn't expect any more from the rest of you."

" Oh, don't be *touchy!*" implored Julie, looking deeply concerned, while Val dived for her hat, which she thought she had hung on its own peg.

" What's all this?" Miss Dymchurch, who was on cloakroom duty, came, with her usual air of charging at full tilt, towards the crowded group.

" My hat's ruined! It was on the floor, trampled and trodden on. That girl took it off my peg and hung her own there." Trembling with temper, Aileen glanced angrily at Val, while the Fifth gazed open-mouthed, too much astonished to gasp. It was used to most things, but not to this.

" Val, what's your peg number?"

" Twenty-three."

" But this *is* peg twenty-three. Are you sure you hung up your hat, Aileen?"

" Of course I did," said Aileen sulkily, tossing her curls.

" There's no ' of course ' about it, as it happens," said Miss Dymchurch sharply. " Lots of people like to fling down their hats on that side seat when they come in—until they discover what generally happens in this overcrowded place."

Aileen pouted, putting the daisy buds to rights.

" Now didn't you do that?" said Miss Dymchurch.

" I may have put it there when I came in, but I'm sure I hung it up afterwards."

" Be surer to-morrow, if you don't want to spoil another hat. By the way, why aren't you wearing your school sailor? Haven't you got one yet?"

" Yes, but it hurts my head."

Aileen expected the explanation to be received with instant understanding and sympathy, as it would have been at home. To her astonishment Miss Dymchurch showed no concern, but merely told her to get another, while the Fifth actually laughed.

" They talk about having to put your hat on with a shoehorn in America," said Julie. " Instead of stating the ailment simply."

" Put on your last shoe with or without a shoehorn," said Miss Dymchurch quite amiably, " or you'll be here after the bell rings and find yourself with a bad order mark."

She charged from the crowded corner and went off to see what the juniors were doing. Julie looked up from tying her shoe.

" Has it ever struck you that you're a sneak?" she inquired of Aileen, dispassionately.

" Hear, hear!" said someone else.

" If I were Val Forrest I'd make it my particular job to see that you were quite cured in a very short time," said Pauline.

Val, who was straightening the bent brim of her

sailor hat, looked up. Aileen, mottled pink with the various emotions through which she had passed during the last ten minutes, regarded her with ruffled dignity from beneath the flowery brim. One daisy, which had come loose during the misadventures of the hat, dangled with comical effect just before her nose.

" You know, if that were my hat, I'd be quite glad to have it smashed up," said Julie. " And next time I'd persuade Mother to get me something *quite* unsuitable for a six-year-old."

" Oh, but it's so *innocent*. So fresh and simple, with its little daisy-buds."

" Just right for the ringlets. How do you make them, by the way? Rags or papers or curling-tongs or what?"

" Does it take long? Isn't it a fag?"

" Fag? It'll be Mother's pride and joy. And isn't the result well worth a little trouble?"

Miss Dymchurch, guessing what was going on, swooped, and the Fifth, who were all ready, hurried out of the cloakroom. Val, who, even when she was a little girl, and had taken part in it, had always felt more shame than amusement in ragging, in the many setting on the one, was thoroughly relieved. As Aileen passed her, with her conceited, mincing little walk, she looked up, drawn partly by that queer instinct which sometimes makes people glance at what they really don't want to see, partly by a real sympathy with

one who, like herself, was a newcomer, cast on an unknown shore. Aileen paused, with that rather pathetic
expression of infuriated weakness which had struck
Val on the first day.

" I *hate* you!" she said, and went on out of the cloakroom.

CHAPTER III

A Pair of Paste Buckles

Walking back to The Turret, Val tried to be amused. She remembered once having gone through a grazing field with a little girl who was terribly afraid of cows, and almost shrieked with fright when a horned head raised itself from the buttercups and looked at her mildly and inquiringly. Having scuttled along in cover of the hedge, climbed a stile, and reached a field where ewes were placidly feeding, she heaved a great sigh. " *Now* let's chase the sheep," she said. " I wonder if the Fifth are Aileen's cows and I'm the sheep," Val said to herself. " It's pretty terrible to be set on like that—I don't wonder she wants to take it out of someone." But in spite of her efforts to explain away Aileen's outburst, she really felt appalled. Even if you don't care much for the opinion of the person who says it, " I hate you " always brings a sense of dismay, rather like that which in the old times sent people rushing off to buy talismans against ill will and the evil eye. " Mrs. Wilby is quite enough just now without a real enemy at school. The other girls I like—but I wonder if they often rag in the Fifth,"

she thought. They didn't, of course, but Aileen's air
of pampered superiority, curiously blended with a
sort of resentful timidity, had been too much for them,
and her complaint to a mistress of another girl by name
had given them the opportunity to express their sentiments. That the complaint was unfounded did not
signify much—what was of importance was that this
mother's pet should learn to fight her own battles.
Val, who had been at school since she was seven, knew
that Aileen's attitude was all wrong, but she couldn't
help feeling sorry for her. " I don't know what I
should do if they all set on me like that," she thought.
" Bear it, I suppose. But I *should* hate it."

Mrs. Wilby was out for luncheon, and, finding no
sign of a meal, Val sought Ashdown, who was, she
said, just having a set down after washing up.

" Anything for me to eat?" she demanded.

" The missus didn't say, Miss Val. She put out my
dinner for me before she went."

" Rake up something for me, will you?"

Ashdown looked doubtful.

" The larder's locked, Miss."

" Oh, I'm so *hungry*."

" I'll tell you what, Miss Val, I'll lend you three-
pence, and you can get one of Alston's A1 pork-pies
from Turrell's at the corner—they're nice and tasty."

" No, no, Ashdown, I won't do that, thanks very
much. I'll just wait till Mrs. Wilby comes in."

Val rushed up to her ugly room, afraid lest the urge of hunger should be too great, and she should accept the threepenny bit she had not, as far as she could see, any prospect of being able to refund. " What shall I do?" she thought. " I simply must get some money. I can't run away and get a situation, Mother would be so worried about it. And I don't want to leave Myra Dakin's. Can I *sell* anything?—Oh, I *am* hungry. People on desert islands tighten their waist-belts—I haven't got one that *will* tighten." She found the girdle of her gym dress and tied it firmly round her waist, hoping to reduce the pangs of appetite. Then she got out her treasure-box of carved aromatic wood, and carried it down to the garden. She felt better, somehow, in the open air.

She took out the string of jagged corals she had worn when she was a baby, a necklace of glass beads which had beauty but was of little value, a gold safety-pin brooch, and a couple of paste shoe-buckles which Mrs. Forrest had removed from her party shoes, substituting plain ones. That was all. She sighed, looking at the small shining heap of treasures beside her on the grass.

" I say, Miss Val, those buckles is *loverly*."

She looked up and saw Ashdown pausing, on her way to the dust-tub with an empty sardine tin, to admire the sparkling things.

" Do you think so?"

She held them up to the light so that they should glitter their very best.

" I like them too," she said.

" I'm going to a swarry to-morrow," said Ashdown, her small childish face eager and joyful. " I'll get away afore Missus and you comes back from Lyncote, so I'm sure not to be 'indered at the last minute. I got a pink Jap silk and some w'ite stockings I 'ad last summer for the Girls' Friendly twinked a treat to match."

Val sat back on her heels.

" What fun! I think you'd look nice in pink silk."

" It's from the Ladies' Wardrobe, of course, Miss Val, but you wouldn't know it'd been worn, well, not 'ardly. And I got some pink roses to wear in me 'air, something like those they sell in the streets on Alexandra Day."

" You'll look jolly nice, I'm sure," said Val, pulling in the gym girdle. " What sort of slippers?"

" Ow, just me old ones, Miss. I couldn't dye *them* pink; well, you couldn't expect it, considering the time I've 'ad them and all, but I've done 'em over with peerless gloss, and perhaps I'll get a bit of ribbon to smarten 'em up."

" How would these do?" Val twirled the paste buckles.

" *Do*. Ow, Miss Val! they'd be all right. You

aren't thinking of selling 'em, are you? I'd give you 'arf a crown, but I expect they'd be more expensive than that."

Val laughed, flushing a little.

" Selling them? No. I don't want them myself. You can have them if you like—if you think they'd look pretty for your party."

" They'd just be the finishing touch! They'd just complete me!" And Ashdown clasped her hands in ecstasy.

" All right—have them." Val put them in her apron pocket. " She's quite pretty," she thought. " What fun she'll have at her ' soirée '. I'd like to be going to a party myself."

The little maid departed in such exultation that she absent-mindedly flung the sardine tin over the wall into the neighbouring garden instead of into the dust-tub. " Ow, well, they can just 'eave it back if they don't like it," she told herself, and went off to her kitchen; while Val, left to herself, chewed a blade of grass and wondered how Nebuchadnezzar acquired his taste for it.

She was half asleep in the sun when she heard a voice above her.

" 'Ere's a bite for you, Miss Val."

Ashdown deposited on the grass a round tin tray, on which were placed an A1 pork-pie, its castellated crust glistening golden brown, a roll, and a glass of

water with a lemonade powder and spoon put in
readiness by it.

" Don't say you won't 'ave it, now," she begged.
" You gave me them lovely buckles; you might let
me just give you a bite o' lunch, seeing as 'ow Mrs.
Wilby forgot to leave you out any, not being used
to you being 'ere yet, like. I'll be that disappointed
if you don't eat it," she added, and Val suddenly
realized that she would, and that it would be not only
difficult but probably wrong to refuse.

" But I'm going to eat it," she said. " You're a
brick, Ashdown, it's the very luncheon I like." And
she set to work to demolish it, and never had anything
tasted better than that pie, roll, and bright yellow
lemonade.

" Ashdown is really rather nice," she thought, as
she devoured the last crumb and drained the last drop.
" The difficulty is—will Mrs. Wilby be used to me
being 'ere, like, ever?"

CHAPTER IV

An Unexpected Meeting

Mrs. Wilby was astonished and grieved to find that Val had had no regular luncheon. She had understood that it was provided in school on Fridays. Dinner was no earlier and no more plentiful than usual, and, if it had not been for Ashdown's timely aid, Val would have gone to bed very hungry. As it was, she found herself looking forward to the possibility of an interesting meal at Lyncote, as if she had been seven years old instead of fifteen.

" I hope it'll be a sitdown tea, with cold meat and pickles," she thought. " It just *might*. How glorious if it were!"

These being her sentiments, she almost clapped her hands when she discovered that they were asked to luncheon, and exhibited so much pleasure and interest that Mrs. Wilby grew plaintive.

" One would think you were not happy here at The Turret, dear," she said.

" But going to Lyncote is part of being here," said Val. " I mean, I shouldn't be going if I weren't living

with you. And it's jolly to be going out on a Saturday
—especially as I'm not playing games."

"Personally, I very much dislike Saturday travel-
ling," said Mrs. Wilby. " I'm not accustomed to it.
But I thought I would make this little sacrifice so that
you might have the opportunity of meeting the Ellertons."

The sacrificial attitude was well to the fore during
the ten minutes spent in the train, but Val, who had
had a notion that she might be asked to produce six-
pence for the fare, which she could not have done, was
so much relieved to find herself with a genuine green
third-class ticket, the gift of Mrs. Wilby, that she was
not too much worried by it. And when they turned in
at the gate of Lyncote she was full of pleasure. A short
drive flanked with flowering shrubs led to a low porch
of golden grey stone, by which the lilacs were already
in blossom. Right up to one side of the house was a
stretch of perfectly kept turf, and beyond it a low
balustrade, overgrown with a tangle of budding roses,
and steps leading to a kitchen-garden, where, in their
time, lupins and larkspur, poppies and sweet-william,
peonies and pinks grew, as well as fruit and vegetables.
There was a smell of wallflowers by the porch. Perhaps it was planted below the windows on the far side
of the house, where a thicket of pink and gold azaleas
was just coming into bloom.

" This is lovely!" Val cried, with a little skip of

pleasure. " Oh, I'm so glad we came. Isn't it a beautiful garden?"

" It is very nice, dear, but don't prance about in
that absurd way. You're rather too old to show your
enjoyment quite like that, don't you think?"

Val did not answer, but composed her steps to the
utmost decorum. She was rapidly forming the decision that Mrs. Wilby was a little mad. " Not dangerous—just to be humoured," she told herself,
feeling that it would be easier to bear the lady's constant fault-finding if she looked at it like that. " Is
she the same with all girls?" she wondered. " Perhaps
Nina has noticed something queer."

The household was evidently at present composed
of Mrs. Ellerton, Miss Ellerton, and Nina. There was
a Captain Ellerton, Val gathered, but he was generally
away from home. Nina was absent too, but this
appeared to be unusual.

" She went into the woods to look for orchids," said
Mrs. Ellerton, a faded, fair woman, who greeted Val
very kindly. " Nina *loves* flowers."

" She won't find any orchids in the woods. If
there are any yet, and there aren't, they'll be in the
marshy place — Paigle Meadow, the children call
it," announced Miss Ellerton, who was dark and
decisive looking, and spoke as if addressing a
meeting. " Come here, child, let's look at you."
She took Val's chin in her hand and turned her face

to the light. " Like her mother—like Rose, isn't she? Pretty girl."

Val felt pleased, but embarrassed. Mrs. Ellerton looked at her in a critical, rather worried way.

" Rose was fairer, *much* fairer," said Mrs. Wilby decidedly. " There's no comparison between a dark child and a fair one, *I* think. Rose was more Nina's colouring. Now Nina always makes me think of a lily —a straight young lily."

Mrs. Ellerton seemed relieved. Val wished the straight young lily would come in and put an end to the conversation, which made her feel shy. But she did not. Luncheon was served—cold lamb and mint sauce, and new potatoes, and a crisp salad, perfectly made; Vienna rolls, and gooseberry tart and cream. " I wonder what Pauline would say if she knew how I'm *loving* this," thought Val, trying not to eat too ravenously. All the conversation was of Nina: Nina's strange poetic fancies, one of which must have come upon her this morning; Nina's graceful movements; her talent for painting and for music; what her dancing mistress had said, and her art master; and why she was advised *not* to take up the violin; Nina's presenting a box of Edinburgh rock, sent by a misguided aunt, to one of the maids—" She can't have expected *me* to eat it, can she really, Mummie? She must know I touch nothing but chocolates." " But the joke was," said Mrs. Ellerton, " that the little rogue had actually sampled it before handing it on to Emma—two sticks were missing. She's just a child still, a lovable child." Val had placed Nina pretty accurately long before the end of the meal. " But perhaps she isn't as ghastly as her mother makes her seem," she thought. " What quaint characters I'm meeting now I'm on my own— the experiences of Alice in Wonderland are nothing compared with mine. I hope Nina *will* come in. I'd like to see her, just for a bit."

However, Nina did not materialize, and, with a little sigh, Mrs. Ellerton told Emma to have a tray ready for her when she did come. " It's naughty of her to be so late," she said plaintively, " but she'll be dreaming in the woods, and won't realize the passing of time."

" Would you like to explore the garden, Val?" said Miss Ellerton. " I don't suppose you want an after-noon rest, do you?"

" I'd love to. Not a bit," and Val ran out on to the sunny lawn.

" Pick yourself a bunch of something, dear," said Mrs. Ellerton languidly, " if you care for flowers."

" There's a trout stream in the orchard, beyond the kitchen-garden," shouted Miss Ellerton, after her. " Do a bit of fishing if you like. There's tackle in the shed."

" Oh, this is lovely, *lovely!*" thought Val. " What pansies—oh! those black ones! I wonder if I really may pick a bunch. Mrs. Wilby'll probably hate me to. Oh, the *orchard!*"

She flung herself down in the long grass by the stream, watching a yellow wagtail pick his dainty way among the king-cups, sniffing the blended sweetness of all the scents that go to make up the essence of May. It was a perfect place. If only she had someone to share it with her—one of the Fifth—preferably Pauline. And suddenly she thought of Ashdown, getting herself up in the pink silk and the old shoes with the paste buckles. " I believe she'd love it too," she reflected. " She'd say it was a fair treat."

She laughed to herself, and then started up, as she heard a little affected cry. And she did not lie back again. For there stood her avowed enemy, the " Mother's pet " who had been ragged by the Fifth, the other new girl, Aileen.

For a minute she was too much surprised to say anything. Then, as the new-comer did not seem inclined to break the silence, she managed to do it.

" Do they call you ' Nina ' at home?" she asked abruptly.

Aileen nodded.

" Silly—it's a silly name, and it's to be stopped now I'm at school."

" Why ' Nina?' ' Lena ' would be more like it."

Aileen looked at her suspiciously.

" I couldn't say Lena or Aileen when I was a baby;

I called myself Nina, and the name stuck. Now tell those horrible girls that, and they'll jeer at me for it on Monday."

" They wouldn't—why should they?" said Val. " But I shan't tell them—why should I?"

Aileen pouted.

" Funny that I never guessed we were coming to see you," said Val. " Never for a moment did the truth glimmer upon me."

" I knew," said Aileen. " That's why I went out into the woods. I didn't want you to come, but Mother had asked Mrs. Wilby without consulting me. She might have put you off, but Aunt Carol was in one of her obstinate moods, and persuaded her not to. But she couldn't force me to have luncheon with you."

" Such a topping meal, too," said Val. " I don't know how you could bear to miss it."

" I shan't miss it. I shall have a tray brought to me directly I go in."

" Bring it out and have it by the stream," suggested Val.

" Why?"

" Because it's such a glorious place."

Aileen gazed at Val.

" Don't you realize that I hate you?—that I simply don't want to have anything to do with you?"

" Well, you've said so once or twice."

" Don't you *care*?"

"Not much. A bit, I suppose. It's awkward to bring out such bursts of hate without at all knowing why."

"You're so smug—so self-satisfied—so conceited."

Val opened her grey eyes wider. She really was astonished.

"Well—now I see all right why you hate me," she said.

Aileen's answer was to burst into tears.

"I don't know whether I do now I come to think of it," she gasped out between sobs. "It's those horrible girls—that hateful Fifth Form—you seem to do everything right and everything I do is wrong—it isn't fair—that's what makes me hate you!"

If Val had been astonished before, she was now fairly astounded. But in all her perplexity and embarrassment she had one very definite desire—that Aileen would stop crying.

"Look here, don't do that," she said. "Your mother'll think we've had a terrific row."

"So we have," sobbed Aileen.

"Well, let's stop it. If she thinks I've been cruel to you, she won't ask me back, and I'd love to come."

"You wouldn't," said Aileen chokily. "You're just saying that. I know you don't want to come. I know it."

"Not want to come back after that salad and gooseberry tart and cream?" was what Val thought of saying, but rightly decided that Aileen wouldn't like it. " I really do, and very much," she said. " I'd love to see all over your garden—and have you any dogs or horses or anything?"

" Dogs," said Aileen in a faint voice. " Spaniels. In the stables. Auntie Carol says they're odoriferous, and won't have them in the house."

" Look here, don't you think you should wash the tears away? There's the stream, all handy. And I'll go up and fetch your tray, and you can have a picnic here under the apple trees."

" Very well," said Aileen.

" Good. Take care—don't get a fish in your eye." Val bit her lip, hoping that hadn't been too facetious. But Aileen smiled feebly.

" The kitchen door is round by the azaleas," she called, as Val ran up the orchard slope. " And tell Emma to send down some marzipan walnuts—then you can eat them while I'm having luncheon, and keep me company."

CHAPTER V

Ringlets

It was pleasant to find Aileen more normal and natural, and Val's genuine delight in the beauty of the garden could not fail to make her more friendly. They explored every corner, and Aileen picked a great bunch of dark pansies, which Val saw in a large old soap-dish which at present adorned her dressing-table, and which she thought must have been relegated to her room because the lid was broken. " They'll make a tremendous difference," she said. " For about five days I'll come home and see them."

Aileen was amused.

" Fancy being so keen on a lot of old pansies," she said. " Why, they grow just like weeds."

" They don't at The Turret," said Val, gently laying her cheek against the glowing, honey-scented bunch.

" I'll give you some more when they're dead," said Aileen. " I can't promise to bring them to school: it's such a fag to carry them. But you can come and get them—and some time we'll play tennis. When it isn't too hot."

Val enjoyed Aileen by herself better than when they were with the others, for Mrs. Ellerton's doting pride, Mrs. Wilby's acquiescent flattery, and Nina's impatient off-handedness created an atmosphere in which it was difficult to feel very happy. However, the afternoon had been a success, and, when she put her bowl of pansies on the ugly dressing-table so that they might be reflected in the looking-glass and enjoyed twice over, as it were, she felt for the first time as if the room were really hers.

But on Sunday morning Mrs. Wilby opened fire.

" Dear child, where is the bunch of pansies we brought home?"

" In my bedroom," said Val.

" Don't you think that is just a tiny bit selfish? Why not put them down here, where we can all enjoy them?"

" I thought there were enough here, and Aileen gave them to me," explained Val, who had carried home an enormous bouquet of lilac, irises, and rhododendron, gathered by Mrs. Ellerton for her guest.

" Gave them to you, and so you keep them for yourself? Somehow it didn't strike *me* to put all *my* flowers in my own room," said Mrs. Wilby smoothly.

" I'll bring them down. But they are so lovely there. I do like them so."

" Don't speak so resentfully, Val. Your mother had

that brusque way, but I can't allow it from you, in my house. Yes—I think you had better bring them down; for your own sake. It is a stuffy unhealthy habit to sleep with flowers in your room, especially if the window is shut."

"But my window isn't shut," said Val indignantly. "It's open as wide as it will go, always."

Mrs. Wilby looked pained.

"Run and fetch the pansies, dear."

Val brought them down, was mildly reprimanded for using what turned out to be a receptacle for sponges as a pansy-bowl, and saw them squeezed in little ornate vases with narrow necks, and dotted in a meaningless way over the furniture of the morning-room. "I don't believe she wants them a bit," the girl thought furiously. "I can't stand it—I can't stand it. If only she'd throw things at me, or slap me, when she's feeling like that, I think I'd be happier."

However, she was happy enough in school on Monday. There was more *Twelfth Night*, and she read Viola; the other lessons went well, and the Fifth, who interested her, showed friendliness, not in any big demonstration, but in the hundred little ways which can be felt more easily than named. Unfortunately, in the same indescribable little ways they showed a sort of mocking disapproval of Aileen, whose attitude towards them was still one of offended superiority. "If only she'd stop trying to impress them with that eye—if she just wouldn't look at them at all for a bit," thought Val. " Poor soul—I wonder if they make her feel as Mrs. Wilby does me."

About the middle of the week she again gave them an opportunity of showing their opinion of her. While tidying her desk—she kept her property in very good order—she used the one next it to the right, which happened to be Julie's, as a dumping-ground for her books. When its owner arrived, it was impossible for her to lift the lid.

" Hullo—what on earth—oh, it's *you*. Having a spring-clean at this stage of term?"

Aileen said nothing.

" Move off your stuff, please. I want to put away my books."

" Wait a few minutes, *please*," said Aileen haughtily.

Julie gazed round at her friends.

" Listen," she said, " only listen to it."

With extreme leisureliness, Aileen continued to stack away her books, now and then, as if on second thoughts, rearranging their order.

" One—two—three—GO!" Half a dozen pairs of hands swept the new girl's property from Julie's desk lid to the floor. Aileen, furious, turned pinky-purple.

" How rude you are!" she exclaimed.

" *Aren't* we?" said a proud voice.

" We are. Oh, we are! Yes, we ARE!"

" We haven't any manners—we haven't—we have NOT!"

" That sort of thing will happen as long as you don't recognize other people's rights to their own desks," explained Pauline.

" *Look* at the ringlets. They're fairly wagging with fury!"

" Give me one! Give me one as a keepsake."

" And me!"

" Or just half a one—half one of those darling little sausage rolls, just enough to put in a locket and wear near my heart."

Some one laid an irreverent hand on a curl, and for an instant Val thought it was really to be cut off. But Aileen jerked it free.

" I shall complain to Miss Dymchurch," she announced.

" Do.   *Do* complain."

" Let me be there at the time."

" We'll say we were acting, as the juniors do—modern method.   Just getting up enthusiasm for *The Rape of the Lock*."

" I suppose you think you're very clever," said Aileen crushingly.

" We do.   We know it."

Fortunately Miss Dymchurch rushed in, her usual air of being at full tilt emphasized by a pair of board compasses and a set square she held like spear and shield. The Fifth settled down to polite intelligent perusal of geometry, and Val looked sidelong at Aileen, to see if she would care for a loan of india-rubber, or some sign of friendliness. But Aileen evidently was not feeling inclined for anything of the sort. However, that afternoon, when the drill lesson was over, she sought Val out.

" You might have stood up for me this morning, I do think," she said complainingly.

" Why?" Val was a little annoyed.

" Why, when those horrible girls were bullying me. You might have said a word to prove me in the right."

" But I don't think you were. I think you were simply asking for it when you pushed that great pile of books on to Julie's desk."

She expected an indignant protest, perhaps another " I hate you ", but Aileen merely looked astounded.

" They needn't have been so nasty," she said, in a small voice.

" No, they needn't," agreed Val, wondering if it would ever occur to Aileen that, while her home people thought her the most marvellous little being, to be coaxed and propitiated in every way, she was of no more account at Myra Dakin's than any other new girl would be.

" They aren't nasty to you like that," Aileen pouted.

" Cheer up! they may be yet—probably will."

" Don't be so sarcastic and horrid. What do you

think I ought to do—complain to Miss Dymchurch? Mummy would take me away at once if she thought I was unhappy—but she didn't want me to come in the first place, and neither did Aunt Carol, and I just know how *she'll* say: ' Well, I told you how it would be '."

" I wouldn't complain to anyone. I'd just lie low. I don't believe," added Val, with more wisdom than she was aware of, " that people ever like anything or anyone new. The thing is to lie low until they get used to you being there."

" I think that's rather hypocritical and sneaky," said Aileen with a very virtuous expression. " Do you think," she went on, with an abrupt change of subject—" do you think that there's anything wrong with my hair?"

" Not really."

" Ringlets are beautiful, you know, only the Fifth are too ignorant to realize it. And it's absurd to say they're babyish, for grown-up girls used to wear them. If they'd read Dickens and Thackeray, they'd know that. But they haven't, they're too utterly ignorant."

" We have an old photograph of Granny at home, when she was about seventeen, with ringlets," said Val. " Mother simply loves it—and really it's rather sweet."

" *Well!*" exclaimed Aileen in triumph.

" But of course curls do go with other things,

don't they? A crinoline, and low neck and short sleeves, and sandals, or those funny little boots. And there's a look, too, girls used to have. I don't think it's any good being ringletty unless you have all the other things too."

Aileen was impressed.

" What do you think I should do? Cut them?" She seized a pen-knife and held up a curl as if about to slice it off, but discretion prevailed, and she put down the knife with a sigh.

" Wouldn't your mother be upset if you did?"

" Oh, Mummy's absurd. She's always raving about my hair being so thick and fine and silky and the rest of it, and lets me in for all this misery."

She gave herself a petulant shake, and then, as Val said nothing, glanced at her interrogatively.

" Do *you* think my hair is nice?"

" Yes."

" Then what would you do with it? Have it shingled?"

Val imagined Mrs. Ellerton's probable horror and grief.

" I wouldn't do that," she said hastily. " But I'd brush out all those curls and tie it back with a bit of black ribbon."

" Well, will you do it for me?"

" Rather, if you like."

They went down to the cloakroom, which happened

to be empty, and Val brushed out the ringlets, tied back Aileen's hair with the ribbon that had adorned one side of her head, and twisted the tail round her fingers.

" That'll give it a nice-looking curl at the end," she said, " and it won't be such a shock to your mother as if there wasn't a single trace of a ringlet left."

" How do I look?"

" Nice. I like it," and Val hurried out of the cloak-room before Aileen, for her expression of gratified vanity was funny, and she didn't want to hurt her too sensitive feelings by laughing at it.

Next morning in school, Aileen looked so much improved by her more grown-up way of hair-dressing, that Val felt quite proud of her handiwork. She had a pretty little head, and some of the expression of pampered peevishness which spoiled her face seemed to have gone with the corkscrew curls. " It's really rather strange that they should have been sweet for Granny, and silly for Aileen," thought Val, pondering the vagaries of female fashion to the detriment of her Latin classwork. The Fifth, too, approved of the change. Someone pretended to shed a few tears for departed beauty, but the demonstration was not popular, and Aileen spent a calm day, in which she might have been any member of the Fifth—Julie, in fact, borrowed her india-rubber, and, after the geography lesson, Corinna asked her if her father had ever come across a shark.

"Train home with me and I'll give you some more pansies," said Aileen to Val at the end of the day. Remembering the fare, Val refused, but suggested that she should walk out on the next day, a half holiday. "I want some exercise," she said. "I used to play games a lot."

"Why don't you now?"

"Oh, I don't know," said Val vaguely. "I may, after half term. Meanwhile, I'm getting flabby. I'd love to walk out to your place."

"There's a private way through Rookmere, much the best. If you meet a keeper, say you're coming here, but probably you won't see a soul."

"I suppose you won't walk home too?"

"It would kill me," said Aileen with conviction, "I'm rather fragile, you know," she added, seeing the astonishment in Val's face.

"Now I hope she won't tell the Fifth that in exactly those words, just yet," thought Val, and, turning out of the cloakroom, ran into Corinna, who seemed to have been waiting for her.

"I say! *I'll* walk out with you," she said, voice mysteriously lowered. "I love ranging over the countryside, and I've never been right through Rookmere in my life, because Father had words with a keeper, or rather a keeper had words with Father about a wire-haired terrier of ours, a perfect darling, who upset a pheasant in some way, and we've all kept clear of the place since."

"Right. I suppose you won't get tired, will you?" Val looked rather doubtfully at the wispy little figure.

"I don't know what fatigue is," declared Corinna. "I've muscles of steel. Feel *that!*" and she rolled up her sleeve and shot out a thin arm, in which the ghost of biceps was visible.

"Ah, but you don't walk with that sort of thing," said Val, adding quickly—"But I'm glad you're coming. It's such a waste to see a lovely place alone."

CHAPTER VI

The Lake in the Woods

Val slipped away unquestioned after luncheon, and was joined by Corinna, armed with a very thick stick, and carrying a satchel of the kind that was in favour with schoolgirls before the vogue of the attaché-case. These articles she introduced with some ceremony.

"My stout ash plant," she said, brandishing the stick with enthusiasm so sudden that Val skipped back a pace. "Not much to look at, perhaps, but a good old trusty friend. And this is my wallet," giving it a resounding smack, "my wallet of victuals to eat by the side of a bubbling stream while I'm waiting for you. Don't let me eat them before we get there if poss," she added in an anxious voice, "or it'll be fearfully dull dangling round by myself."

"But won't you come up to Aileen's place?" said Val. "I'm sure she'll be glad to see you."

Corinna shook her head.

"Can't be done," she said darkly. "You can't

insult a person's coiffure one minute and accept her hospitality the next."

" All right. I'll carry the wallet when you begin to feel ravenous," promised Val. " What have you got in it?"

" Oh, a hunk of bread, and a lump of cheese, and a billy for tea."

" How nice!" Hunks and lumps seemed to Val just then the ideal way of serving food. " Oh, Corinna, is *this* it? Oh, what luck! Oh, isn't it glorious—no, not glorious—but isn't it heavenly? No, it isn't heavenly, 'cept the bluebells—it's earthly, one of the special earthly places, like the forest where the sleeping beauty was."

The two girls had turned in at an old black gate which led to a broad grassy drive, nibbled short by rabbits. Light fell in lovely patterns on it between the leaves of the great overshadowing beeches, and here and there was a tuft of pale violets. On both sides were glades of uncurling fern, and the blue of the wild hyacinths crept among the fronds like smoke from some magical, incense-burning fire. Now they passed a cluster of the delicate white stars of the stitchwort, now a big mossy stone where wood-sorrel grew. In the distance the blossoms of rhododendron glimmered among dark leaves. Somewhere a stream sang away to itself. " It's hidden for a bit, I believe," said Corinna. " But soon it shows, and then we come to the place where it runs into the lake."

" A lake! Is there a lake?" cried Val.

" Yes, the mere, you know. Rookmere."

" Of course." Val walked in ecstasy. She had loved the garden at Lyncote, but she loved this wood-way better still. It seemed to be hers, hers and Corinna's, they were finding it out, and any moment they might come across some lovely thing that hadn't been planned by anyone, that hadn't even been seen before. The failure of Marraby's and the gentle disagreeableness of Mrs. Wilby seemed small things that didn't matter, any more than did the facts that Val's midday meal had been a very meagre one, and she had only a halfpenny, a franc, and a shoe-button in her purse. And Corinna was a good companion. Whatever her physique might be, her will was indomitable, and, as Val guessed, served her as well as brawn and beef might have done. And obviously she adored the place, loved being out.

" *Games!*" she said with scorn. " I wouldn't be smiting balls about for anything when I might be here."

" I must say I like smiting balls," confessed Val.

" But you like this *best*?"

" Well, I wouldn't change it for anything just now," said Val, with a deep sigh of pleasure. " Oh, Corinna, *look!*"

They stood on the borders of a dark and shining lake. Opposite was a white shore where the straight young oaks, planted at regular intervals, showed green and gold against massed foliage of a more sombre kind. The flat leaves of water-lilies floated in a shallow stagnant bay to the left; the flowers were not yet out. To the right were bushes of bird-cherry, and an old black boat, broad in the beam, was roped to a wooden fence that ran out into the water. The thwarts were at such a distance that it was possible to lie curled up between them, and a scattering of hay, and a piece of tarpaulin, suggested that someone had slept there for the night.

" You might camp there," said Corinna. " You could get one of those special boat-covers, a hood thing, to sleep under, in case it rained in the night, and lie out looking up at the stars."

" Which you wouldn't be able to see, unless the cover were perforated," said Val practically. " But, Corinna, one could *live* there."

" Of course."

" Imagine living there—living there for the whole of the summer holidays. What money would you want? Something for food, of course. How *does* one earn money?"

" It would be great sport," said Corinna, looking at Val. " Are you going to do it? I suppose you'd have to get permission."

" I wonder if one *could*. Permission and money—money and permission."

Corinna was a little surprised at the eager serious way in which Val spoke.

" If you *do* camp anywhere you might ask me to come too," she said. " I've got a billy-can and a box of matches, anyway, and I don't think Mother could have any reasonable objection to my removing the blankets from my own bed."

" Oh, I'll ask you, if I can get as far as that," promised Val. " I'll—hullo, Corinna, what's that?"

There was a movement in the hay that was scattered in the boat, and a fox terrier pup, barking wildly, leapt up. Planting his forefeet on a thwart, he looked at them for a second, and barked once more, stopped, looked round, and barked again. Apparently he didn't quite know whether he wanted to keep these interlopers in their proper place or to express his own feelings, which were not cheerful. Finally he resolved on the latter course, and, flinging up his head, uttered a long sad howl.

" That was what poor old Nib was like," said Corinna. " Funny—our family seems doomed to fox terriers in this place. I hope it isn't his ghost come to warn us of evil in store."

" *That's* too young to warn anyone of evil," said Val. " He's just a baby. Keep calm, James. Hold on a minute, and I'll be with you."

Climbing on to the shaky fence, she stepped cautiously along its middle bar, and jumped into the boat. The pup abandoned his sense of duty, and greeted her with rapture. Evidently he was lost, frightened, and lonely, and Val's hands and voice were comforting.

" I wonder he didn't jump overboard and swim out," she said.

" I expect he didn't feel like it. All dogs can swim, but not many do," said Corinna. " And this is terrible water, deep, deep, dark, and cold. They say there are secret springs and whirlpools in it, and, if you went in, you might be dragged under and drowned."

" In that case, we won't drop you in, will we?" said Val to the puppy. " Just snuggle up and don't jump, and we'll have you safely on shore in no time."

The pup, shivering from the end of his nose to the tip of his tail, just to show how badly he needed sympathy and encouragement, obeyed, and Val carried him safely across to the bank. Then she put him down on the grass.

" Go home!" she requested.

The pup looked at her and wagged his tail.

" HOME, SIR!" said Corinna, in what was meant to be a voice of thunder.

The pup rolled over on his side and put one paw over his face.

" It's no good trying to be firm with *that*," said Val. " We'll have to take him along with us and trust to finding his owner somewhere in the wood."

" Right. He can keep me company while I'm waiting for you," said Corinna, nothing loath. And Val felt quite sorry to leave her, when, having helped to make a bright little fire between two stones, and set the billy-can on to boil, she turned to see her curled up by the spring at the edge of the wood, happily chewing part of the hunk and the lump, and from the rest concocting a sort of Welsh rarebit for the pup, whose tender years seemed to demand something moist and melted.

Aileen seemed glad that she had come, and gave her tea exactly where the tray luncheon had been eaten, under the apple trees by the trout stream.

" Aunt Carol was disagreeable about it, of *course*," she complained. " She wanted us to have it by the azaleas, because this is a longish way for Emma to carry out the things. It's so *silly*. What are maids for, I'd like to know?"

" Corinna would enjoy this," said Val, wishing that the wispy girl, whom she was beginning to like very much, could be one of the party.

" Corinna?"

Val explained that Corinna was eating bread and cheese and minding a pup on the edge of the Rook-mere estate. Aileen looked sulky.

" I don't know why you should think of dragging her out with you," she said.

" I didn't. She came."

" I like you, but I hate the other girls. And Corinna's such a freak, too. Never mind. She needn't spoil our enjoyment."

Val saw that it was useless to hope that Aileen would offer Corinna hospitality, and, incidentally, show herself in a more attractive light to one of the Fifth. She changed the subject, but after tea said that she had better go, and come again to play the single Aileen proposed.

" Corinna will be sick of waiting. Besides, it'll take some time to walk back."

" Go and tell Corinna *not* to wait any longer. We'll run you back in the car later."

Val looked surprised.

" Oh, well, *go*. But I shan't give you any pansies."

" You're a baby!" said Val crossly. " I can't help it. You must see that it would be horribly mean to let Corinna trudge all that way home alone. It wouldn't be so bad if she hadn't waited."

Aileen said nothing.

" Well, good-bye," said Val.

Still mute, Aileen stared in the opposite direction. There was nothing for it but to go, and, feeling hot, cross, half right and half wrong, Val walked off. But before she had reached Corinna's camping-place she heard the sound of racing feet, and, stopping to look back, saw Aileen galloping after her.

"Here!" she said. "I didn't mean it about the pansies." She thrust a great dark sweet bunch into Val's hands. "And," she added, "here's a rose; it's for Corinna."

CHAPTER VII

Exit Ashdown

Val and Corinna agreed that it would be a sin to force the pup to spend a night in the police station.

"Perhaps you had better keep him for a bit," said Corinna. "Tiger Tim might kill him."

During the afternoon Val had heard of some of the exploits of the big fierce tom belonging to the Shaws, and she was ready to agree that it might be better for him and the pup not to meet. "But I don't know if I can take him," she said doubtfully. "You see, I'm not living with my own people, and I'm pretty certain that Mrs. Wilby wouldn't care for him."

"Couldn't you smuggle him into the garden secretly, and hide him in an outhouse of some sort? To-morrow's Saturday, you know."

"I don't think it's easy to keep a pup a secret. I might ask Ashdown. She might have a friend who would put him up just for one night. But if there isn't an advertisement for him in the paper to-morrow, to the police station he must go."

However, when she reached The Turret, Val found Ashdown too busily engaged in controversy to be asked about lodgings for a pup. As soon as, with a discreet tap, she had let herself in, she heard Mrs. Wilby's voice from the morning-room, and, in contrast with its smooth annoyance, an occasional sniffle and yelp of unrestrained indignation from the little maid. Under cover of this, she ran up to her room unnoticed, wrapped the pup in an old Burberry, besought him not to move or speak, and fetched him a saucer of watered milk. As she went downstairs she heard her own name, and, one hand on the banister, stopped to listen.

"As if Miss Valentine would *give* you things of that sort! Why, the girl is not well off—she is in poorer circumstances than you are."

"They aren't real dimints, though. They're paiste. Miss Val said so when she gave them to me."

"I don't expect people in your position to realize the value of old paste," said Mrs. Wilby coldly. "In any case, that is not the point at issue. To ask you to restore the food you have so greedily pilfered is useless, sorry though you may be——"

"I ain't sorry!" burst in the small shrill excited voice of Ashdown. "If you'd only forgot and left the key in the lock I'd 've 'ad out that tinned tongue afore this! For the last month I ain't 'ad enough to keep a mouse going, let alone a Christian."

" It really doesn't signify to me whether you're sorry or not," went on the level tones. " But what does signify is the loss of Miss Valentine's property. You will bring down those buckles at once, and put them here, on this table, before you leave this house."

" Leave it I will, certingly," retorted Ashdown. " I wouldn't breathe this air another night. But give back them buckles I won't, unless Miss Val wants them off of me. I'd give 'em to her in a minute. But she gave 'em to me, and she wouldn't go back on me in any court of law and say she didn't."

Realizing with horror that a dreadful mistake had been made, Val burst into the morning-room.

" She's right, Mrs. Wilby! It's all right! I gave them to her—for the swarry, the soirée, you know. The day before we went to Lyncote, it was."

If she had expected her guardian to rejoice at the clearing of Ashdown's character, she was at once disillusioned.

" You weren't listening at the key-hole, surely, Val?" said Mrs. Wilby in gentle surprise.

" No. No. I was coming downstairs and I heard there was a row on—I mean, I heard you both talking."

" There is no ' row ' on that I am aware of," said Mrs. Wilby, acidly.

" If you look round a bit perhaps you'll notice one," muttered Ashdown.

Mrs. Wilby lifted her eyebrows. There was a moment's silence.

" I gave her the buckles—I just had to tell you that," said Val.

" Dear, as your informal guardian, I can't countenance your giving away what little valuable property you have. I blame myself very much. I should have taken charge of it directly you came here."

" But these buckles aren't valuable, really," protested Val. " They aren't old paste at all. They were on a pair of slippers Mother bought for me in some London shop, I forget which one, and she thought they were too showy for a schoolgirl, and got a plain kind to put on at home instead. I remember quite well, because I wanted to wear the sparkly ones so badly."

" Exactly."

" Really, honestly, they *aren't* old paste," repeated Val, feeling more hopeless than she had done since she was a baby, trying to make grown-ups realize how right she was and knowing they never would. " Why, slippers and all only cost about two guineas."

" I'll give 'em back to you, Miss Val, w'atever they cost," burst out Ashdown. " It's 'er that annoys me. I don't see w'at it's got to do with 'er or anybody else."

" No, no. I don't want them back. I gave them
to you and you're to keep them," said Val.

" That ends the matter for the present," said Mrs.
Wilby. " Please go up to your room, Ashdown.
I will come in while you pack your box."

Ashdown stumped upstairs with emphasis, particularly pronounced when she reached the uncarpeted
top stair leading to the little garret rooms apportioned
to herself and Val. Mrs. Wilby looked reproachfully
at her ward.

" Dear, do you think it quite wise or kind to take
the part of my own servant against me?"

" I didn't mean to take her part against you,"
said Val miserably. " I heard what was going on—
I couldn't help it, and I simply had to tell you that
you had made a mistake if you thought she had stolen
the buckles, and that they were valuable——"

" No actual mention of stealing was made, with
regard to the buckles, except by the girl herself,"
said Mrs. Wilby quickly. " An accusation of that
sort cannot be made lightly. Please remember that,
Val, if you intend to bear witness against me, which,
apparently, is your plan. In the matter of the
tinned tongue, of course, the girl was caught red-
handed."

" Oh, it *isn't* my plan." Tears prickled in Val's
eyes. She knew quite well that Mrs. Wilby's in-
sinuations could be worse than bald statements, but

the idea of giving evidence against her was somehow a dreadful one. Suddenly she felt tired out and lonely. "Oh, I'm so unhappy," she said. "I don't know what to do."

Mrs. Wilby regarded her.

"Try to be more tactful. If you had anything to say about your gift to Ashdown, surely it would have been better to wait till she was out of the room."

"Perhaps it would," owned Val.

"Well, dear, I think it would be wise if you ran and fetched what other valuable trinkets you may possess, and I'll lock them up for you. We do not want a repetition of this sort of thing."

It was evidently impossible, thought Val, to convince Mrs. Wilby that the buckles were of no value. She fetched her little box of treasures, and handed it over. For a second she had thought of keeping back the beads of coloured glass, but had put away the notion. She would be asked if she had brought everything, and there would be more fuss.

Mrs. Wilby looked inside the box, and her lips tightened. Val wanted to say: "You see, I have nothing that's any good," but she felt so tired that to placate her present guardian seemed the most desirable thing in the world.

"This is all?"

"Yes."

"You will sleep in the pink room to-night, please.

I do not want you to be troubled with communications from that girl."

Realizing that her new quarters were on the ground floor, behind the morning-room, and that it might be possible to take the pup for a run before going to bed, Val tried to summon up enough good spirits to congratulate herself on her luck. And certainly she was lucky in that the presence of the pup was not discovered. The behaviour of Ashdown engrossed the thoughts of Mrs. Wilby, and she had no ear for the two or three small but shrill yelps of excitement that Val could not persuade her charge to control. In the morning Ashdown departed, carrying her own luggage, a Japanese basket and a round cardboard hat-box. Mrs. Wilby stood by Val's door, as if to prevent any sudden egress for purposes of farewell. "Not that my saying good-bye would do any good," thought Val. "But I'd like to know what she's going to do." She watched the small figure, at once jaunty and pathetic, staggering down the gravel path between the box and the basket, both swinging and impeding her movements as if they had some ill-will towards her. "Perhaps she'll turn, and I'll wave good-bye." But Ashdown, who had evidently planned a dignified exit, did not turn, and, going out with chin well tilted, left the garden gate wide open. Tucking the pup under her jumper, Val softly turned the handle of the door, peeped out, and, seeing the coast

A DIGNIFIED EXIT

clear, bolted up to her own room. There, on the
dressing-table, was a letter for her, on pink scented
notepaper.

" Dear Miss Val—

      " this is just to say oh revoir and
to explain that mrs wilby was furious because seeing
she ad left the key in the lock I took the libberty of
making a mele off the tinned tung and dry old stuff
it was seeing as ow it as been in the house for a long
time for visiters as did not turn up as if they would
no they had too much sence. Good-bye dear miss
Val and I wish you was out of it too I know of a place
I think and a place as is one and not a dog kennel
minuss the dog biskitt no more at present but I hopp
we shall meat again as something seems to tell me
may be

            " yours Sinseerly

                " Gladys Ashdown."

" It's more of a dog kennel than she knew, isn't
it, James?" said Val to the pup, as she folded the
letter and slipped it in her pocket, trying to forget
that she felt lonelier than ever now that Ashdown
had gone. " Now we'll go off to the free library and
find out if there's anything in the paper about a small
dog lost."

Mrs. Wilby had gone out to consult a friend on the

subject of a respectable charwoman. Val made the beds, washed up the breakfast things, and did a little dusting of the flick - round sort. Then, with that glorious sense of freedom that always came to her with escape from The Turret, she ran out on to the white road, curving between lime trees towards the square where school stood, and the town hall, and the brick building of the public library. Luck was with her. The space before one copy of the *Dakin Priors Post* was actually unoccupied. Eagerly glancing down the " Lost and Found " column she saw:

" Lost, fox terrier pup, black patches on head and back. Answers to name of Spang."

Val decided not to put this to the test in a public reading-room.

" Reward. Seyton, Thornytangle."

" I shan't forget that name. I wonder if it's the house, or a little village." She was turning away when the name again caught her eye, in the middle of the second column, for " Situations Vacant ".

" Wanted. Latin coach for boy of seven, one hour daily, any time. Mrs. Seyton, Thornytangle."

That a boy of seven should learn Latin did not at once surprise Val. What struck her was that her Latin would be sufficient for the purpose of teaching him. She liked small boys, having had some experi-ence of them during former holidays spent with a lively family of them. And one hour daily—*any* time.

" It's Providence," she told the pup eagerly. " Or "—with the human instinct not to tempt fate by being too sure—" it *may* be."

CHAPTER VIII

Val gets a Job

Thornytangle, the young librarian, with nothing to do at the moment, told Val, was beyond Tinkers' Dell, so called from its ancient history, for tinkers weren't allowed to camp there now. "It's just the one house, and a row of cottages. You can't mistake it," he assured her.

She knew the whereabouts of Tinkers' Dell, as during the Rookmere walk Corinna had pointed out a lane leading to it, and in half an hour found herself by a little wicket gate set in the middle of a thick hedge of sloe, dog-rose, and blackberry. A thorny tangle it was indeed, and it seemed never to have been pruned or cut since it had begun growing. Val liked it. It reminded her of the picture in her old fairy-tale book of the thicket that grew up round the castle of the sleeping beauty. "The Turret is dull," she thought, "but everywhere else I go seems specially interesting. I wonder what will happen here."

She lifted the latch, and went along a paved walk, bordered with tufts of yellow stonecrop and masses of pale purple and rosy pink rock-garden flowers whose names she didn't know. At the end of the walk was a wide porch, where the door, standing hospitably open, showed a pleasant white square hall, with a low bookcase, a broad cushioned settee, and a grey stone jar of apple-blossom. She had not time to ring the bell before there was a wild howl of relief and delight, and a small boy in a jersey dashed upon her, seized Spang, and hugged and kissed him until it seemed as if, rescued from his wanderings, he had come home only to perish from excess of affection.

" Mums! Mums!" shouted the happy owner at last, " come quick. Here's a girl who has found Spangie, and brought him home."

Mrs. Seyton, as Val judged her to be, ran out at once. She was attractive to look at, tallish, with dark shining hair, and her face was so sunburned that her eyes seemed extraordinarily blue.

" Don't say ' Here's a girl ' like that, Sam," she commanded, pulling her small son's hair quite hard.

" She *is* a girl," he retorted. " Why not? She's a nice girl," he added, looking at her with mischievous eyes, blue as his mother's. " But a girl all the same."

" Where did you find the pup?" asked Mrs. Seyton.

Val told of the boat on the dark lake at Rook-mere.

" That's Tom Soutar's doing!" shouted Sam.

" I'll punch him! I'll pound him to a jelly! I'll give him a black eye!"

Mrs. Seyton looked slightly worried.

" Sam quarrelled with these Soutar boys while they were playing near the Rookmere woods the other day," she said. " But surely they wouldn't be so horribly mean as to put a tiny pup alone in that boat——"

" Tom Soutar would! I know him! He's a black-hearted rascal! Let me come at him, and I'll show him——"

" Don't be ridiculous, Sam. You know you're only seven and he's thirteen. You must take better care of your pup in the future, and not mix yourself up in quarrels with these big boys. Well," she turned to Val, laughing, " I suppose you'll have an orgy of macaroons and strawberry-ices?"

She opened a leather pocket-book and drew out a clean crisp treasury note. Val flushed. Again she was being offered money. Poor Ashdown had wanted to buy those buckles; Mrs. Seyton wanted to reward her for finding the pup—and very badly did she want the subscription for the Myra Dakin games. But she shook her head.

" Oh, that's all right," she said. " I'm glad I happened to come across the pup. He's such a darling."

Sam stared at her in amazement.

" Aren't you going to take the reward?" he said in awed tones.

Mrs. Seyton laughed again.

"Now *do*," she said. "We're so much indebted to you—and what's the use of sending you a small present you don't want? People of your age can always spend a few shillings to very great advantage."

"I don't want it, really," said Val, pink as the blossom in the stone jar. "But, if it isn't filled, and I'm not too young, I'd love to apply for the Latin post."

"The Latin post?" Mrs. Seyton looked puzzled for a moment. "Oh, yes, to teach *Sam*. He goes to a kindergarten, but his father believes in the civilizing influence of the dead languages, and maintains that when the boy begins Latin he'll cease to be the particular type of nuisance he is at present."

She looked thoughtfully after Sam, who had rushed off to get food for his puppy, and then regarded Val.

"You *are* a bit young," she said. "But, of course, he won't be able to learn much—just enough to know what Latin is."

"I'm nearly sixteen," said Val. "I'm good at Latin, rather. I'd love to do it. Couldn't you try me for a week or a month, and see how he gets on?"

"*Well*," said Mrs. Seyton, considering it. "What's your name, by the way?"

"Valentine Forrest."

"You are so much like a girl I used to know. Rose,

her name was, Rose Faukner. We were at Myra
Dakin's together, once."

"That's Mother," said Val, looking down at the
garden walk. Suddenly her throat felt salt and sore,
and the cracks between the stones seemed to become
very wide, and moved about queerly. She clenched
her hands tight, and, when she looked up again, she
was not crying, though her eyes were full of tears.

"Father died five years ago, and we lost our money,
most of it, when Marraby's failed, and Mother has
gone to Montreal to live with distant relations, sort of
cousins, old people, who wouldn't be bothered with
me. They sent for her all of a sudden, and she
thought she must go at once. She hasn't seen where
I live. But she's having a good time, she rides on the
Mount nearly every morning, and she loves that,
and——"

A sob broke out in spite of her efforts to control it.
Mrs. Seyton's arm went round her shoulders.

"But she'll be back here to see you soon, of course
she will! And what luck that we've found you out!
Why, Tom Soutar ought to have a reward of some
kind for hiding the poor pup, instead of the black eye
Sam talks about so nobly—when Tom isn't there.
Dear, of course you shall have the job! Though I
don't know if you'll like it—but you shall have a free
hand with Sam, spank him or do what you like with
him, I shall be quite ready to believe that he deserves

it. Why, of course you're good at Latin, Rose used to
beat us all—a clever, clever girl, and so charming to
look at——" She ran on, and her kindness, so heartfelt,
so free, seemed to Val almost divine.

" Wilby—Mrs. Wilby are you living with? Isn't
that another of your mother's old friends—Florence
Hicks? The Turret? I'm not sure of the place. It's
fairly new, isn't it? I don't often go to the other side
of Dakin Priors. I'm lazy, I'm afraid, and I love
this part of the world too much."

" Yes, she was at Myra Dakin's too," said Val. She
was not sure if she wanted Mrs. Seyton to call. She
was beginning to have a queer nervous dread that Mrs.
Wilby might make her appear to other people what
she seemed to be at The Turret: clumsy, boorish,
insolent, ungrateful. " Of course it's very, very good
of her to have me," she added, fearing lest her tone
had betrayed her feelings.

" It's nice for her, too," said Mrs. Seyton. " Well,
Sammy on Monday at four. Will that do?"

It did beautifully. Val calculated that it would take
less than half an hour to reach Thornytangle from
Myra Dakin's, and school ended at half-past three on
Mondays. She left the place with a light heart, walking as easily as if her feet had wings. Ten shillings a
week—it was more than pocket-money, it was an
income! She would be able to join the games club, to
buy herself something to eat when she was hungry,

to give any subscription that might be asked for in school. She could help Ashdown if that character were in distress. She could pay back Mrs. Wilby for what was being done for her. Couldn't she leave The Turret? No, she couldn't do a big thing like that without asking her mother.

"I wonder if Mother would mind," she thought. "I wonder if the Hunnikers would think I ought to stick it out. Oh, I *hope* I'll be able to teach Sam! I won't say anything to Mrs. Wilby till I know if I can. How glorious it is to have a job! Oh, I'm glad—glad—glad!"

There seemed no limit now to what she might be and do.

CHAPTER IX

Bad News and Consolation

There were letters from Canada that night, one from John Hunniker for Mrs. Wilby, and one from her mother for Val. Val's was very short, and it was written in pencil—Mrs. Forrest hated writing or receiving letters in pencil. Val read it, flushed, and turned pale.

" Mother's ill," she said to Mrs. Wilby. " She says it isn't much, that she's really just tired, and will be quite fit soon. Is there anything at all about it in your letter?"

Mrs. Wilby laid a soft, rather warm hand on Val's.

" My poor child!"

" Oh, what? what?" cried the girl in agony. " Let me see your letter—oh, tell me quick! What is it?"

" Dear, you mustn't be hysterical!" said Mrs. Wilby, her smoothness a little disturbed by the terror in Val's voice, which she hadn't expected to be quite like that. " There is nothing to disturb yourself about, nothing at all. Of course you shall see the letter: the part that

relates to yourself." She tore off a half sheet. " It is
nervous breakdown, dear, a very natural thing after
all that she has been through these trying months.
There are limits to the endurance of all of us, and
perhaps your dear mother is not amongst the most
robust. She will have every care and attention with
the Hunnikers, who appear to be very wealthy people,
and can well afford to give her the best."

Val seized the half sheet of Mr. Hunniker's letter,
and devoured it eagerly. What Mrs. Wilby said was
quite true. There was no cause for alarm, the old man
insisted, none whatever. A period of rest and freedom
from worry would put everything right. " She really
should receive no correspondence for a short time,"
he ended, " but I think that she would be so much
distressed not to hear from her daughter that the
omission, though recommended, might do more harm
than good."

" You have not been writing worrying letters, I
hope, dear?" said Mrs. Wilby.

" No, no! I said I was happy—I told Mother about
the garden at Lyncote, and how I was playing Viola
in *Twelfth Night*, and the names of the girls I like in
the Fifth."

" You must be very, very careful. Young girls
are apt to exaggerate their small troubles, especially in
strange surroundings, little realizing what harm they
may do."

" Mrs. Wilby! You don't mean that I have made Mother ill!"

" Did I say so? Don't be so hasty and so theatrical, dear; don't forget that I am very much grieved about poor Rose myself, for she and I were friends in the old days. It is sad, Val, as one grows older, to see one's friends going——"

" Mother isn't going!" cried Val emphatically. " She wouldn't, she simply wouldn't be *dreadfully* ill right away there, away from me: she just wouldn't do it."

" It's very nice to think so, dear, but at nearly sixteen we must try to face facts."

" I am facing them! But I'm going to face facts, not nightmares!" The girl gallantly tried to give herself the courage that Mrs. Wilby seemed to wish to drain from her. " I'll write to Mother now, at once, and I'll write to Mr. Hunniker too. I know he dislikes everyone under thirty, but I expect he'd make allowances for me now, and send me just a postcard to say how she is."

" I'm sure he'll do that, dear," said Mrs. Wilby gently. " Just bring down the letter and I'll slip it in with mine. You'll exercise self-control in writing to your mother, won't you, Val? Perhaps I should just glance over your letter—an older woman understands——"

" Oh, no! I *will* be careful. I'll hardly say anything

but how much I love her." Tears slipped down Val's
cheeks. " That couldn't hurt anyone——"

" It might. So much depends." Again the soft,
warm hand pressed Val's. " Dear child, I am truly
sorry for you, and I want to help you, but you *are* a
little difficult, you know."

Val said nothing, but she did not withdraw her
hand from the caress. She wanted to like being at The
Turret; she wanted to like Mrs. Wilby and to feel
proper gratitude towards her. If only she had been
more like Mrs. Seyton, or the energetic shouting Miss
Ellerton, or Miss Dymchurch, or Miss Sylvester, or
any of the mistresses at school. What *was* it—what
was wrong with her? " Or is it wrong with me?"
thought Val, as soon as her anxiety for her mother let
her consider the less important question of the relationship between herself and the friend to whom
her mother had entrusted her. " There *must* be something nice about her when Mother liked her," she
thought.

Certainly there was one point, Val decided, in Mrs.
Wilby's favour. That was the amount of freedom she
very willingly allowed her. School ended at half-past
one, or, on " late days ", at half-past three, but Val
did not seem to be expected to go home then. In
Ashdown's time, a cup of watery tea and a slice or
two of bread and margarine were occasionally put
in the morning-room at five o'clock: on the day of

her departure, and the one following, Mrs. Wilby was out and nothing was left for Val. On Monday, when she returned from Thornytangle, where she had had tea, she was not questioned as to her whereabouts between four and six. " It might mean hunger," she told herself, " but it doesn't. It's an act of Providence in disguise."

She thoroughly enjoyed going to Thornytangle. Sam, on discovering that the first declension went *mensa*, *mensa*, *men*SAM, seemed to regard Latin as a personal compliment, and gave it his earnest attention. He had a good memory, and enjoyed learning things by heart, if he could do it in his own way, which was sometimes by shouting his lesson to the time of a march round the room, sometimes playing a declension game with Val, with a death for every case missed, sometimes saying mysteriously— " I'll tell you a secret!" and whispering what he knew of the last noun, the singular in one ear, the plural in the other. He was very restless, and very lively; but Val didn't object to these qualities, and, when she received her ten shillings on Friday, counted the money easily earned.

It was on that day that she made an astonishing discovery. As she went down the flagged walk, de-lightfully conscious of the weight of four half-crowns in the pigskin purse that had been empty for so long, she felt that someone looked at her, and turned to where a small neat figure in rose-coloured linen, with white cap and apron, crossed the little lawn, carrying a laden tray. It did not pause, but one dark eye gave a prodigious wink. Val almost cried out with surprise. It was Ashdown.

" *She's* all right!" she thought with happy relief, and hurried back to school. Tennis would be in full swing now. She could not wait till to-morrow to make herself a member of the games club. She must find Pauline and pay her at once.

" Hul-lo! So you've swopped the stamp collection for the stuffed owl?" said Pauline.

" Something like it," Val laughed happily. The smell of the closely shorn grass, the whiteness of the newly marked lines, and the new balls against the green, the familiar cries—" Well up!—Out!—Gone away!—Thirty all!—Vantage in!"—all were very good after what seemed a long exile.

" D'you want a game now?"

" I haven't shoes. Oh, but my gym ones are in school, of course." She ran helter-skelter for the cloakroom, happy and excited as if she had been seven years old.

" But I didn't put down my name." She stopped in the middle of tying a shoe-lace, and her face fell, as she saw four players stroll up to the only unoccupied court.

" I put down mine, though. Go ahead," and Pauline

handed over a racket whose glossy strings proclaimed it new that season.

" Thirteen and a half—that's my weight." Val swung it delightedly. " Oh, Paul, are you sure you don't mind?"

" Go on," said Pauline laconically.

The others looked a little anxious when the game began, for Julie was one of the first couple, and Becky a substitute player, but Val played at the top of her form, and their fears gave way to approbation. " Don't forget to put down your name, every day," said Julie, and Val, laughing and delighted, promised two nights a week.

" But why not a set every evening," asked Pauline, walking home with her. " You don't live far from Myra Dakin's—prep won't take you all afternoon and evening too, will it?"

" No. But there's a big slice out of my time already." And Val told of Thornytangle, and Sam's Latin lessons. Pauline looked at her with wonder and re-spect.

" What's he like? I shouldn't care much to be an outsider tackling my young brother Thomas," she said.

" He's rather nice—jumpy, of course, and tries to be funny a bit too much, sometimes. His mother's a darling." Val's voice suddenly lost its eager excited confidingness. " What a brute I am," she said, angrily.

" I didn't think I should ever stop thinking about Mother till she was well again. And I've been as keen on that tennis as if I'd had a letter saying she was all right."

" What's wrong?"

Val quickly told what she knew. It was easy to tell Pauline things.

" Look here, my uncle and aunt are going out to Montreal in a few days—he's a doctor and attending some big medical conference there. If you give me the address of the nursing home where your mother is, I'll get them to call and find out at first hand how she's getting on. They'll be jolly glad to do it. You had better come to tea and meet them. If she has got to the stage of having visitors, I expect she'd rather like to hear about you from someone who had seen you quite recently."

" Oh, Pauline! Do you think it could really be managed?"

" Of course. It's obviously the thing to be done. They're only there for the conference—but they'll have time to see her once at least. Conferences leave lots of margins."

" It's very decent of you." Val's heart grew so much lighter that she realized that, though she had jerked it away from her, her anxiety had lain heavily on her even during the tennis.

" And she'll be all right, you know," said Pauline.

" Uncle Richard is by way of being a specialist in nervous complaints, and it's almost incredible how completely people who are really very, very ill recover."

Val felt further comfort. " How funny it is that Pauline should want to be a Stoic, and to bear everything without caring or complaining, when she makes other people so much better," she thought, after they had said good-bye at the gate of The Turret. " I hope she'll fix a definite time for me to meet that uncle and aunt. I hope she won't forget."

And the good thing was she knew Pauline wouldn't.

CHAPTER X

Corinna changes her Mind

The days became longer and sweeter, and the trees shutting off gardens from the road were suddenly bunches or shower bouquets of blossom: hawthorn, lilac, laburnum. The road-sweepers swept up piles of lime flowers with the dust, and all the streets smelt of flowers and new-cut grass. Corinna, always a restless wisp, fretted continually at the restriction of indoor life, though, with casement windows flung wide on to the garden, bowls of fresh flowers in their form-rooms, hours of tennis or swimming in open-air baths, the Myra Dakin girls did not fare too badly.

" But it's all measured out," said Corinna, when Julie reminded her of this. " I want to be *free*. I want to tramp along the open road, and drink at the spring, and sleep under the stars, with my wallet under my head for a pillow, and my stout ash plant——"

" To drive away cows," said Julie with a shudder. " Oh, for a deck-chair in the River Gardens, with nature under proper control, and a band."

"I'd like the open road too," said Val, who had a good deal of sympathy with Corinna, and a conviction that, unlike many rhapsodists on the joys of the free and simple life, she would carry on quite happily in bad weather as well as in good.

"Tewkesbury Road," said Corinna. "I'm learning *Tewkesbury Road* for my own day to-morrow."

"My own day" was the day on which the Fifth learned poems they chose for themselves from the poetry shelf in Miss Sylvester's room.

"I'll learn it too," said Val. "I nearly know it, anyway."

"How many lines has it?" inquired Julie.

"Twelve."

"Twelve—it might be managed. Read it, Val, and I'll take it down."

"Here's a Masefield," said Pauline, who always carried a book of poetry in her school bag.

"It is good to be out on the road, and going one knows
    not where,
Going through meadow and village, one knows not
    whither nor why;
Through the grey light drift of the dust, in the keen
    cool rush of the air,
Under the flying white clouds, and the broad blue lift
    of the sky."

"Keen cool rush of the air!" said Corinna, opening

and shutting her mouth like a small fish out of water.
" Isn't it a nice poem?"

" And to halt at the chattering brook, in the tall green
      fern at the brink,
  Where the harebell grows, and the gorse, and the fox-
      gloves purple and white;
  Where——"

" You know, I shouldn't learn that poem," said
Pauline. " It's dated, it's hopelessly dated."

" I love it," said Val.

" Love away, but don't expect Tewkesbury Road
to *be* like that. That was written long before charras
were thought of, motor ones. Tewkesbury Road!
If you learn that poem and believe it for to-day,
you're filling your mind with delusion, and Plato
says——"

" Speaking of filling, I have a basket of cherries in
the cloakroom," said Julie. " Go on copying for me,
Val, and I'll fetch them. I don't think they're exactly
ripe, but they may be better than nothing."

The cherries seemed to put Plato out of Pauline's
mind, and Val and Corinna were allowed to learn
one of the prettiest of out-of-door lyrics without
further comment or criticism. But she had not finished
with them.

" Corinna?" Miss Sylvester was in an open-road
mood herself on the morning of the next delicious

day, and she knew that Corinna would have learnt
a poem of out-of-doors.

Corinna said one verse, and Val one, and Julie
one, and the class approved:

" Three of you learned the same poem? Did you
all feel like that?"

" I know a poem of the same kind, with a difference,"
observed Pauline.

" Come along—let's have it—Twelve line limit,
though," said Miss Sylvester, and Pauline began:

"ANY ROAD, BY ANY WALKING TOURIST

" It is ill to be out on the road, going one knows not
    where,
Going perhaps to heaven, perhaps to the village close
    by.
Through the petrol-fumed drifts of hot dust, while the
    hoot and the toot blast the air,
And the bottles crash out through the hedges, and the
    shouts smite the terrified sky.

" And to halt at the tin-bestrewn brook, in the glade
    where the party had tea,
Where the orange-peel lies, and the boxes, and news-
    papers, pink 'un, and white,
Where the fire for the kettle was kindled at the roots of
    the bark-blackened tree,
Where flowers torn up without pity lie dead at the
    coming of night.

" O, to hear the honk of the charras, and the yells, and
  the squalls, and the mirth,
It's a tune for progress to strut to, achievement past
  power of words—
But the rose-rifled hedges are voiceless, and there's not
  a sweet place on the earth
For the man who walks with his pack on a road without flowers and wild birds."

" Oh!" said Miss Sylvester. " Well, what do you
think of that?"

" Give her eight," said Julie.

" It's a *shame!*" declared Corinna. " It isn't like
that—it isn't half as bad."

" It *is*," said someone in the back row. " Look
at Tinkers' Dell!"

" *Don't*," said Pauline.

A discussion, with the usual punctuation of " Yes "
and " No " and " 'Tis " and " 'Tisn't " followed.
They were asked to express their sentiments about
parody, which they were nothing loath to do. Corinna,
especially, was so certain that it was a mistake that
Pauline, as if repentant, after the lesson was over,
and the conversation turned on sleeping out, had
a suggestion to make. Val had already noticed how
ready she was to give people what they wanted: had
it been possible to produce the wild mustang and the
pampas-covered plains for Corinna, she would certainly have done it.

" Well, why don't you sleep in ours?" she said, as Corinna bemoaned the fact that there was hardly room for Tiger Tim to turn round in their garden, and that a person sleeping in it would feel as if in a grave. " There's plenty of space, if there's nothing much else, and nobody will disturb you."

" Yes, and then you'll write a poem about me in my sleeping-bag," said Corinna. " I know you."

" Have you got one? When? Oh, you simply *must* use it," said Pauline, fired at once. " You can't let a thing like that run to waste. Come along and sleep in our garden any night you like—you needn't spoil the camping effect by coming up to speak to any of the family first: just go ahead with the bed in the bush with the stars to see."

" It would be lovely," said Val. " I'd come with you, Corinna, only Mrs. Wilby would think me crazy if I suggested it. And I haven't any blankets or ground-sheet, and I don't suppose there'd be room for me in your sleeping-bag."

Val's enthusiasm mollified Corinna.

" Thanks, Paul," she said. " P'r'aps I will. Your garden's really a nice tangly place—it's next best to the genuine open country."

" You can be just as uncomfortable in it, anyhow," said Julie. " There's Pauline's young brother Thomas to take the place of the usual fauna—all complete."

Pauline's young brother Thomas was the matter

(D 503)   7

of melancholy comment from Paul herself and most of her friends, but Val liked him. He was just ten, with a nose that was going to be beaky, and hair that always rose in an obstinate little crest at the back of his head. He was surprisingly thin, and his favourite adjective was " powerful ". Val saw more of him than she did of the others, for Roddy, who was fifteen and very shy, would, after a few minutes of resolute but rather strained conversation, proclaim—" Well, I'd better melt away now;" and Angela, the perfectly beautiful baby, who at present showed no sign of developing the family beak, was either in bed or on the point of going there when Val, after Thornytangle, would go along to do Latin translation or history revision with Paul.

" You might help me to-night, Val." One warm evening Thomas broke in on the events and dates of George III. " I've got a nice little job. You'd love it."

" ' 1808. Convention of Cintra.   1809. Battle of Corunna. Sir John Moore slain. Talavera.' What is it, Tommy?"

" Bait. I'm going fishing to-morrow. You dig for it after dark with a 'lectric torch."

" Not mine, take note," said Pauline

" Well, a bit of candle then, and it's good fun. *Do*."

" Worms?" said Val, and shuddered.

" Go and do it yourself now," said Pauline. " You know Mother won't let you stay up late."

" She will. It must be after dark—or twilight, anyway. That's when the powerful ones come out."

" I can't, Tomkin," said Val faintly. " I'll do lots of things with you, but not this."

" Are you frightened?" said Thomas, with sparkling eyes. " Do you hate worms?"

" No. She simply adores them," said Pauline quickly, and with decision. " But she's very busy— *we* have to do homework, you see; we can't slack round as you and Roddy can."

At the mention of homework Thomas looked slightly worried, and he strolled off without further invitation. Various bumps and bangs and rattles from the room above suggested that he was overhauling his tackle and finding a bait-can, and Val sighed with relief.

" Hope poor old Corinna doesn't choose this evening for sleeping out, just after Thomas has been turning up our territory," reflected Pauline. " I think I'll keep an eye out for her and show her a safe patch if she does."

" He can't turn up all of it. I say, Paul, it's getting dark. I ought to go home."

" Roddy'll take you to your gate. Didn't you say Mrs. Wilby wouldn't be back from Sylcote till nearly eleven?"

" Oh, yes, that'll be all right, if Roddy doesn't

mind," said Val, wondering if the youth could manage the whole distance to The Turret without threatening to melt away.

"Well, Father will. He likes a bit of exercise before bedtime. Come along—let's run through American Independence."

Their labours were broken into by the sound of a shrill voice from the garden.

> "The animals came in two by two—
> There's one more river to cross——"

"That's my young brother Thomas," said Pauline unnecessarily. "He always sings a bit when he's alone in the dark. I suppose it does *him* good."

Val looked out. A small figure was scouting about the neglected lawn, in the ring of light from an electric torch. She wondered if she should ask if this were Pauline's, but a certain sympathy with Thomas down there in the gathering darkness made her decide to let well, or ill, alone. The girls worked on, until a sudden squeak followed by a dash and leap of footsteps on the stairs, made them look up. Thomas tumbled in.

"There's a burglar," he whispered hoarsely, "creeping about in the bushes. I heard him."

Pauline glanced at Val.

"You needn't get the wind up. That's just Corinna —Corinna Shaw, you know. She's coming here to sleep out."

" It isn't Corinna," panted Thomas. " It's a burglar—a powerful man. I saw him."

" *Saw* him?" said Pauline incredulously. " Are
you certain, Thomas? Are you *certain* you waited to
see anyone?"

Thomas really couldn't bring himself to say yes, so
he just nodded.

" Well, it is Corinna. And you might go down
and advise her to sleep in the hammock, as you've
heaved up the garden and made it all wormy."

" You come," said Thomas uneasily.

Paul went to the window.

" It *is* Corinna. Look, Thomas. That's her sleeping-bag, all strapped up. I said I wouldn't disturb her,
so that it would seem like real wild sleeping out, and
I said I'd keep the family off, so that she might feel she
was in the real spacious country, but I don't believe
she'd mind you just mentioning the hammock."

" Perhaps she'll help me dig the rest of that bait,"
said Thomas, who was prone to attach himself firmly
to Pauline's friends. " I'll go and see."

" Don't freeze on and be a bore," said Pauline.
" And don't forget to tell about that hammock."

Thomas disappeared, with new confidence born of
the sight of Corinna actually crossing the garden, and
the girls returned once more to their history. They
were just about to stop work, and Pauline was wondering if Roddy or her father were available as an escort

for Val, when a piercing yell came from below, followed by a squawk of triumph.

A door smartly opened.

" What's that? Who's there? Thomas, what are you doing?" Mr. Lankaster's voice came from below.

" Get a light quick, Paul! There's something wrong."

Paul, discovering that her flash had disappeared, bolted downstairs, and, very speedily, lit a candle lantern that always hung outside the kitchen door. The two girls ran to the most secluded part of the garden, where, between two bent old apple trees, the hammock was generally slung. But it was not there now. Mr. Lankaster, a few paces away, clicked on his torch and held it up. The round of light illumined a strange group. Under the string hammock, caught like a bird in the nets of a strawberry bed, struggled a small boy among a scatter of unripe gooseberries. On one side of the hammock knelt Corinna, hands pressed well into the anatomy of the unfortunate youth, while Thomas, with the expression of St. George having slain the dragon, sat on his feet and drew the network round him until he became hopelessly entangled.

" What in the world——?"

" We've got him, Dad! Corinna and I! We've got him!" cried Thomas. " Shall we carry him to prison? Call a policeman, Paul. Go on. Not a moment to be wasted."

"All right, Paul. I'll deal with him." Mr. Lankaster took the net from Corinna and hauled the boy out. He began to howl so dismally that Thomas looked perturbed.

"You're the fruit thief, are you? Now stop crying, and just come along with me. I shan't kill you this time," and Mr. Lankaster urged the delinquent towards the house, while Val and Pauline eagerly questioned Corinna about the adventure.

Thomas had been right. There had been a burglar, though hardly a "powerful" one, in the garden. Corinna had noticed him skulking among the gooseberry bushes as she and Thomas arranged the hammock for a comfortable night's rest. She had whispered to Thomas, and told him to pretend he saw nothing, and what he must do. The two had unslung the hammock, and, suddenly, and with a good deal of skill, flung it over the crouching thief. His accomplices, waiting on the other side of the wall, had basely fled at the sound of his howl of alarm, and left him to the mercy of two captors who, though of small size, were of great determination, and did not mean to let him go.

"I thought at first it was Roddy ragging," said Corinna. "I was going to give him a poke with my ash plant when I saw he was too small, and had the wrong kind of cap on."

"Well, I'm sorry about it, Corinna," said Paul.

" I really meant you to enjoy your sleep out—it was Thomas's bait that would spoil your night, I thought."

" I caught a powerful fish, didn't I?" chuckled Thomas. " Not a worm wasted, either—— There's Dad. What did you do to him, Dad?"

To the disgust of his younger son, Mr. Lankaster had evidently dismissed the culprit under the first offender's act. " He won't be round again for a bit," he said, with a little smile. " But, if sleeping out was your plan, Corinna, I think you had better sleep in, after all."

Corinna looked round thoughtfully, and held out her hand as if to test the atmosphere.

" Well," she said, " I don't mind a little rain, of course, but my sleeping-bag's new, and it does feel as if it meant to *pour* to-night."

CHAPTER XI

A Game of Tennis

Val began to feel that pleasant sense of security and power which comes when, in a game or a phase of life, you " find your feet ", as people say, and know what is going to happen next. The Turret was dreary. Always there was a feeling of not-enoughness there, not enough to eat, not enough to look at, or read, or enjoy in any way. But Val was no longer Viola wrecked on the unknown shore; she had made friends, she was welcome at Lyncote and at Thornytangle, and at the tall narrow house, ugly outside, happy and jolly within, where Pauline lived. She liked her school work, and could do it; she played tennis regularly, and enjoyed it; her earnings for the Latin she taught Sammy gave her a new independence. She sent ten shillings to Montreal, with a shy little polite note begging the Hunnikers to spend it on flowers or fruit for her mother; she kept another ten towards a fund which in her mind she labelled " The Florence Wilby "; she bought small necessary things, such as stamps and toothpaste, on which, in the old days, she had never thought of laying out money—they always seemed to be there. Two things weighed on her mind —her mother's illness, though the anxiety of this had been somewhat lightened by a terse reassuring business note from Mr. Hunniker; and her Thornytangle secret. Every day she wished more heartily that she had told Mrs. Wilby of this at once; every day it seemed more difficult to broach the subject. At last she marked a certain June Tuesday with a red circle in her calendar, vowing that on that day she would explain that, for part of her time, she was a Latin coach, and offer what then might be the accumulation of the Florence Wilby fund towards the defrayal of her expenses. Whether Mrs. Wilby was really hard up she was never certain. " I *wish* I knew why she wrote to Mums and asked to have me," she would think. " She doesn't like it—she can't—but she *did* bring it on herself." And the phrase " a generous impulse, bitterly regretted ", appeared before her mind's eye in print, as she had seen it in some book. " That must be it—or she must feel she's nursing a viper in her bosom, me being the viper," she decided. " It isn't that she dislikes girls, as Mr. Hunniker does— she's enthusiastic enough about Aileen."

It was while brushing her hair that Val meditated on this apparent liking of Mrs. Wilby's, and that very morning at breakfast time the subject of Aileen was introduced.

" I visited the Ellerton's yesterday, dear," said Mrs. Wilby, and then paused, teapot in mid-air, to watch the new maid, remarkable to Val for having the smallest eyes and the largest face she had ever seen, as she set down the bacon-dish, and a rack containing four fingers of toast. " Remove the cover, please, Cooling." Two fragments of bacon were exposed, and one fried egg, which Mrs. Wilby allowed herself, by medical advice, she said. " Poor Mrs. Ellerton was rather upset, I could see at once, by what you did to Aileen's hair."

Val was so much surprised that she accidentally ate half her allowance of bacon at once, instead of making it last and eking it out to the last precious fragment.

" But I've seen her heaps of times since, and she didn't seem to mind! Aileen asked me to do it—the Fifth ragged her a bit, you know."

" ' Heaps of times.' Yes, dear, I rather wanted to speak to you about that, too. Don't you think it rather a mistake to visit Lyncote so often—hasn't it ever struck you that you might be—well, to put it very mildly, somewhat of a nuisance?"

" I don't go there nearly as often as Aileen asks me," said Val, with perfect truth, for her time during the week was fully occupied, and on Saturdays and Sundays she was often with Pauline or Corinna or both.

" Well, dear, doubtless the child has generous hospitable instincts, and, of course, she probably knows how you are placed——"

" How *am* I placed?" said Val suddenly. She didn't know what made her say it: she was astonished to hear the question, and to realize it was hers. She had had no intention of saying anything of the kind. Mrs. Wilby looked at her queerly.

" Surely it is entirely unnecessary to ask that, Val?"

" Well, I'd like to know quite definitely," said Val, with hot cheeks. " I mean—I loathe being dependent, and all that. I know my school fees are paid——"

" And you would like to see your weekly accounts here, I gather?" said Mrs. Wilby smoothly.

" No, of course not, but——"

Mrs. Wilby finished her egg.

" Dear Val, I am sorry you have spoken like this," she said. " I do not wish to emphasize to you, for Rose's sake, the cost, the wear and tear, of keeping a big growing schoolgirl in the house: I do not wish her ever to realize, especially at this time, the inadequacy, the total inadequacy, of what she is able to contribute towards your support."

" I know. But I don't like it. I'm sorry about it. Couldn't I go somewhere else?"

" Suggest the place."

" I can't at present—but supposing somewhere turned up——"

" We will consider that when the occasion presents itself. I am sorry that you cannot content yourself here, Val, very sorry, especially for your mother's sake."

" But I'm all right, really, it's just that——" Val wanted to say " Do you want me to stay or not? Can you bear me or can't you?" but she couldn't put it quite like that.

" Just that—what?"

Val shook her head.

" Well, well, dear, we'll say no more, no more at all." Mrs. Wilby patted Val's hand. Then, drawing out a stout little purse with silver clasps, she produced a shilling. " You can treat Aileen to an ice at the café," she said, with a kind look. " But remember, dear, what I said about visiting the Ellertons. You and I will go there together on a little state call soon, but these casual droppings in—well, dear, you would really do well to believe an older woman, and one who sincerely wishes to be your friend."

It would have been a good opportunity to explain that she didn't need the shilling, and why, but it was twenty to nine, and the Thornytangle tale would have meant being late for school. Feeling that it was impossible to come to an understanding with Mrs. Wilby, Val took up the coin, murmured thanks, kissed the cheek which was offered with a gesture of resigned kindness, and, once beyond the garden gate of The Turret, bolted down the road as if she were escaping from prison. She would be in time, but running relieved her feelings. She only wished the distance were greater. A mile or two, and she might feel normal again.

In the cloakroom she encountered Aileen.

" Val, I shall have to miss my train to-day. I've a returned lesson in English—it's a shame: Miss Sylvester hates me—and I must call at Forbes's for my racket; it's been restrung. Have tea with me at the café."

Val hastily reviewed her afternoon. School ended at half-past one: on " early days " she went to Thornytangle at three.

" I can't come before half-past four. And I'm playing tennis at five."

Aileen pouted.

" You've never had a game with me. You might come out and play on our court."

" Why don't you play at school?"

" School! It's always school. I want singles, just you and me by ourselves. Scratch your name, Val. Come out this evening. *Do!*"

Val hesitated. Aileen burst into querulous complaint.

" You are mean, Val. I do think you're mean. You're so taken up with those horrid girls in the Fifth

that you *never* have any time for me. I don't suppose
one of them cares twopence for you, really, and I do,
and yet you won't come out to Lyncote and have a
decent game with me, on a decent court. It's hateful
for me. You don't know how lonely I am."

"Look here, Aileen, I wish you'd join the school
club. Come to-night, and see how you get on. I'll
speak to Pauline about it. If you don't like it, you
needn't come again. But I'm certain you will."

Aileen maintained the silence which seemed sulky,
but which, as Val had discovered, was sometimes a
sign that she was thinking things over.

"Come and have an ice with me at half-past four,
and then we'll go straight up to school. There'll be
a place vacant in our set—Corinna has sprained her
wrist. She wants to practise with her left hand, but
I don't suppose we shall let her do that for more than
one game. You and I'll play Pauline and Julie. Don't
you think it would be rather good fun? Do come,
Aileen."

"I suppose I must." And Aileen, with the air of
one who is deeply injured, went slowly up to the
form-room.

There were two cafés in the Avenue, the fashionable street of Dakin Priors—the Oriental and the Blue
Paroquet. The Myra Dakin girls liked the latter,
which Pauline described as a quiet little effect in jazz
and dazzle. At half-past four Val looked in for Aileen,

and, not finding her, went on to the Oriental, where, among Eastern screens and blue jars and rushes and fans and beads and gongs, rather older people were wont to drink coffee and consume more solid and nourishing meals than those usually served at the Paroquet. Aileen was not there. But, as she shyly made her way out between the two lines of bamboo tables, Val saw a back that she made haste to avoid— the back of Mrs. Wilby.

Mrs. Wilby was not drinking a casual coffee or eating a casual strawberry ice; Mrs. Wilby was having a meal. Iced cider sparkled in her glass; before her was a plate of salmon mayonnaise; and, as Val very quickly stole past, she looked up from the menu card she had been studying to order lamb cutlets, and pêche Melba. Val's first sensation on reaching the door was one of self gratulation on having got out unseen; then a welcome thought occurred to her. "Why!" she told herself, "she can't be terribly hard up." Lately she had been haunted by the fear that she might be almost ruining her present guardian by making bigger inroads on her resources than that lady, on her first charitable impulse, could have thought possible. It seemed as if that bugbear might be dismissed. She was so much relieved that she nearly ran into Aileen, who was standing outside the Blue Paroquet with her racket, inclined to complain a little at having been kept waiting, but, Val was glad to find, making no attempt to persuade her to give up the school tennis and come out to Lyncote.

" Do you play much at home?" asked Val, as they strolled towards the court where Julie, obviously much bored, served to the left hand of the enthusiastic Corinna.

" Oh, I don't know. I have to play with Aunt Carol, and it's really no fun. She keeps you up to it, and is so cross if you forget the score. It's more like a lesson than a game."

" Pauline and Julie are pretty strong stuff, so we shall have to play up," warned Val.

Aileen turned the white rabbit eagle look, as Val called it to herself, upon the two, who were engaged in chasing a most reluctant Corinna from the court.

" You can fag balls," said Pauline. " You can do that as well with your left hand as your right, and, if undertaken in the proper spirit, it'll be splendid practice for tennis itself."

" I'm not going to fag in the moon-daisies for anyone," said Corinna, quite unperturbed. " If you send the balls in there I shall just go home."

" Oh, stay!" besought Julie in a low voice. " I expect this game'll be worth witnessing."

She glanced to where Aileen sailed to her place on the court.

" Fifteen love she can play," said Pauline. " The grass at Lyncote's the best in the country."

Pauline was right. Without the vivid brilliance that sometimes appears in a schoolgirl's tennis, Aileen's game was a good one. Her drives were swift, low, and hard; she sometimes brought off a quite effective little screw serve; she was evidently used to difficult returns, and didn't muff the unexpected. Her aunt's insistence on the rigour of the game had evidently borne fruit, as it was bound to do. Her faults were a very strong tendency to poach, and an eagerness, sometimes unjustifiable, to proclaim a doubtful ball out if it belonged to her opponents, in if she or Val was responsible for it. However, those did not manifest themselves too blatantly during the first two sets, good close sets, of difficult keen exciting play.

" I wish we could have the conqueror," said Julie, when the second was ended. " But our time's up, I'm afraid."

" Court 3 is empty. Those people skirmishing on it are waiting for this one," said Val.

They looked at court 3, which was newer than the others, and, partly owing to the passionate affection a family of moles appeared to feel for it in spring time, partly to the extreme languor with which the Third, whose special care it was, rolled it in summer, was not levelled to the perfection demanded by good play.

" Is that really a tennis court?" inquired Aileen.

The others laughed, quite pleased with her.

" Let's finish on it. It would be rather a rag," said Julie.

" Can't we ask those people to play on it, and finish here?" said Aileen. " It wouldn't make much difference to them—they haven't begun properly yet."

" Ask them," said Julie. " Ask them by all means. I'll look for that lost ball in the moon-daisies while you do it."

Aileen made a little sound of petulant exasperation.

" Let's toss," said Val. " Heads, we finish on three —tails, we go home, like as we lie."

Heads won. Aileen at once made for the west of the court.

" Toss for sides," said Pauline.

Val and Aileen lost, and faced the sun, always oddly baffling at this time of the evening, when, in his descent towards a wooded hill in the west, he seemed both to glare and glint in a most hostile and irritating way.

" Bad luck!" called Julie cheerily. " Change half-time, of course."

" When we've lost the game," muttered Aileen.

Val and Aileen won the service toss, and Val, having served, prepared to take the back line ball she guessed the return would be. Aileen sprang before her, attempting a net volley, missed it, and glanced back, with a " Your ball." Val made a gallant attempt to get it up, but the glare of the sun, and the interposition of Aileen's arm and racket, made her miscalculate, and she drove it straight into the net.

"Love fifteen!" announced Corinna, who, sitting on an upturned biscuit box, had evidently decided to umpire for this set.

" She won't do that again, anyway," thought Val.

But she did it until the score was love forty. Then she pouted.

" You *are* muffing the balls, partner," she said. " Is it the sun, or what?"

" The sun's not so bad," said Val. " It's you. Don't poach, and we'll climb up."

Aileen stood still, swinging her racket. Val won the next two points. Then Julie smashed a return to the left of Aileen, who made not the slightest attempt to take it.

" Gone!" cried Corinna. " Old girls one—new ones none."

Julie served. Aileen returned the service well enough. It was all she took. During the next game, she served, and then stood idle. At last Val, in exasperation, swung to the left to get a ball which would have been an easy return for her partner, and, getting it up, won the point, as neither Pauline nor Julie, expecting Aileen to leave it, was in time for it. Aileen turned to Val, pouting.

" Don't poach!" she said. " Why don't you practise what you preach?"

" Take your own balls, or try to, and I won't,"
snapped Val.

They changed sides. Perhaps because she now
felt that she was even with Val, perhaps owing to the
relief of playing with her back to the sun, Aileen's
game at once improved. The score of the two new
girls ran up; when it was again time to change the
score stood at three all.

" Cheers!" said the umpire with beautiful im-
partiality. " Play up, old Fifth, play up, new ones."

They needed no encouragement. It was one of
those matches that are contested as keenly as any
played in public between rival schools. Balls rose at
totally unexpected angles from clods of unlevelled
earth and tussocks of unmanageable grass, and the
combatants did gymnastic feats of wonderful brilliance
and agility, and took them. " If only the air could
record the patterns we've made in it," said Pauline.
No one knew whether a serve would be a slither or a
screw, or a rise in the gentle kindly beginner's style,
inviting pat-ball. " I've never seen less monotonous
tennis," said Corinna. " It's here the school matches
ought to be played, not on 1 and 2." Long deuce
games they were, and when at last the score stood at
five all it was no longer a penalty to face the west.

" It's getting dark. Someone will be along to tell
us to buzz off home," said Julie.

" Long set or sudden death?"

" No use trying to play a long one."

" Better to end it quickly," agreed Val.

Aileen said nothing. The set began.

Fifteen all—thirty all—thirty forty—deuce. " Now don't be too dogged about it," cried the umpire. " You can't be found here playing at nine to-morrow morning, and I do want to know how it's going to end."

Aileen served, and Pauline sent back a clever line ball.

" *Out!*" cried Aileen in triumph.

" In, surely!" said Corinna. " What do you think, Val?"

" I thought it was in," said Val.

" It seemed in from here," said Pauline. " But perhaps I didn't see it with an absolutely unprejudiced eye."

" I saw the chalk rise," declared Corinna.

" It was out," said Aileen, with the wronged and haughty look.

" Four against one, counting the umpire," said Corinna cheerfully. " That ball seemed to me in. Vantage in. Hurry up, Paul. Serve."

Pauline served to Val, who returned a long swift drive which rose from a bump at so unlooked for an angle that it was by a pure fluke that Julie got it up. Aileen did not run back or attempt to take what was a clumsy and fairly easy lob. She stood still, nonchalantly swinging her racket.

"Game!" cried Pauline and Julie, with no exultation in their voices.

"Yes, that's game," said the umpire. "And what's the good of me, I'd like to know?"

"So should I," said Aileen.

Not one of the Fifth seemed to have heard the remark.

"Topping set, Val." Pauline first, then Julie, shook hands with her.

"You'll probably be a sub. player," said Corinna. "I'm out of the running for that, of course, with this wrist."

As Corinna's tennis was the mildest and most equable pat-ball, the wrist was hardly necessary to disqualify her from school matches, but her friends nobly refrained from pointing this out. Pauline unscrewed the net and turned it over.

"Played off your handicap yet?" she wanted to know, and, taking Val's arm, walked her off the court. Julie and Corinna followed, wondering if their mothers would allow them to do their home lessons that night, speculating on the chances of success in getting up early to finish them, and stating, without much conviction in their voices, that everyone in authority would agree that it was good for girls to be out all the evening playing tennis and enjoying the fresh air. Aileen was left standing on the court. If she had an expressive gesture ready, there was no one to see it;

if she had much to say, there was no one to listen to it; if she wanted to maintain a dignified silence, there was no one to regard it. Always at home she had felt that the situation belonged to her. Even Aunt Carol's mild and transient severities did not count, as she could rely on so sympathetic and absolute a champion in her mother. These girls, the hateful Fifth, had simply assumed that she had refused to play up, and had deliberately chosen to lose the set. Even if their assumption was right, they had no business to make it. They did not know; they could not prove it. That wasn't the sporting spirit. She would have liked to tell them so—but they weren't there to be told, and wouldn't be there till to-morrow morning, which probably wouldn't afford any good opportunity. She stood there thinking of them, Pauline, beaky and self-contained; Julie, fair and open-faced, her expression always changing; wispy little Corinna, colourless and somehow charming: and she longed to make them care, to make them realize how very much she disliked them. Worst offence of all, they had taken Val with them. Val was different—Val was get-at-able in some way they were not. She would just let Val know. She rushed after them, saw the group separate at the corner, and breathless, followed Val to the curved road that led to The Turret.

" Stop!" she called out. " Val—Val—stop!"

She thought for a moment that Val would hear

and refuse to turn back. But Val swung round and stopped. Aileen would really have liked to slap her, but, standing still, drooping a little after the hard game, and yet, for all her weariness, with the Viola look the Fifth would always see in her, she was singularly unslappable. Aileen seized her by the wrist and gave it a tug.

" I hate you," she said, in a low voice. " I *hate* you."

" You've said that before, you know," said Val. And she laughed and went away.

CHAPTER XII

Good-bye to Thornytangle

It was with mixed feelings that Val went to school next morning. Aileen had certainly made it easy for her to fall in with Mrs. Wilby's suggestion and not to visit Lyncote for some time; but she was sorry that they had quarrelled. Perhaps because, arriving at Myra Dakin's as new girls together, they had read the *Twelfth Night* scene and been laughed at together; perhaps because, for all her angry outbursts, Aileen had been unable to avoid getting on with Val, giving her the pansies she liked so much, wanting her companionship, asking her advice about things—whatever the reason, Val had a strong sense of belonging to Aileen, of sharing with her, the feeling on which friendship is always based. When she thought of their picnic meals by the trout stream at Lyncote, the hair-dressing in the cloakroom at school, the arguments about the Fifth, and Aileen's little sudden surrenders, as on the evening when she had run after her with the rose for Corinna, Val felt that they could not really be unfriendly, saying " I hate you " and scoffing at one another—it seemed too absurd. Aileen would recover. Her way of showing it might be rather trying, but most certainly things would soon be all right, and, after listening to a tirade against the Fifth, perhaps accompanied with tears, Val would be restored to her former position. She wondered if Aileen would ever see—if she did really know that the Fifth had liked her at the beginning of the game, and that her sulky refusal to play up when things were against her had been asking for the sort of treatment she got. " Of course she won't own it," she thought. " I won't say anything about the Fifth—I won't try to coax her to like them until she does it of her own accord. She's sure to, by and by."

But Aileen gave Val no opportunity of coaxing her or talking to her about the Fifth or anyone else. She avoided her all day, and, at the lunch interval, joined some Fourth Formers, for whom a box of expensive chocolates she had brought to school was sufficient passport for entrance to a small recess by the platform in the gym, where, for some reason, they had always sat, or played games that seemed the more violent on account of the cramped space available for them. Her attitude towards the Fifth was that of someone who expects criticism, and is ready to deal with it. But the Fifth, apparently, had finished with her. They did not rag her; they did not pointedly avoid her, as if they saw her and didn't want to. They simply did not

seem to know she was there. They had other things
to think of. It would really not have been surprising
had some one put a few books down on her, or stood
on her to open a window, so completely unrecognized
was her existence.

Val's day went pleasantly. Another of Mr. Hunniker's formal postcards announced that her mother's
health was improving; Miss Sylvester talked of rehearsals for scenes from *Twelfth Night* with which
the Fifth Form, untroubled during this happy year by
public examinations, proposed to entertain the jaded
Sixth, and perhaps a larger audience, at the end of
term; Mrs. Seyton seemed more than usually friendly,
and Sammy fairly gobbled up his nouns of the fourth
declension; evening prep did itself, riders coming out
as if they couldn't have done anything else, and a
French prose covering two pages of her exercise book
as if she had been a French schoolgirl whose star turn
was composition in her own language. "It's just as
well that my luck's in," she thought, "for I shall
want it to-morrow, every bit of it." To-morrow was
the day with the red ring, the day when Mrs. Wilby
was to be told of the Latin at Thornytangle, and
was to be persuaded to approve thoroughly of the
scheme.

"I don't know why I should feel that this is so
difficult," she told herself, walking slowly towards
The Turret at the end of morning school on the red-

circled Tuesday. Things had not gone so well as on the previous day, and Aileen's crossness worried her. It was different from what it had been before. Val was not one of those people who are stimulated by a good quarrel. Occasionally, like every human being with spirit, she was involved in one, but she did not much enjoy it at the time, and hated dragging it on afterwards. The atmosphere of angry resentment of which she was conscious as she worked next to Aileen in class stifled her spirits as stuffy or thunderous air seems to stifle one's breathing power. Besides, Aileen herself was obviously miserable. If all the phrases expressing banishment—turning the cold shoulder, sending to Coventry, and the rest—were put together, they would not sufficiently express the complete in- difference of the Fifth to the girl they had been quite willing to take on at tennis only a few days ago. " I don't know how she stands it," thought Val. " Brace up, now—come along in to luncheon—Mrs. Wilby is a kind soul, really, and one of your mother's old friends. Imagine what Aileen's putting up with from the Fifth."

Mrs. Wilby met her at the front door.

" Before you have luncheon, Valentine, I should like to speak to you for a few moments in my snuggery."

Val's heart went down like a plummet. What was wrong? It couldn't be—it *couldn't* be that her mother was worse. Blindly she followed Mrs. Wilby into that lady's private retreat, the " snuggery ", in which, as far as one could see, it would be impossible for even a cat or a puppy to find a place in which to be snug.

" Mother? I suppose Mother's all right?" she said, in a voice which came queerly because her throat was so dry.

" All right? Well, that is rather an optimistic way of describing her present state of health, perhaps. But, if you mean that you hope no further news has come of your mother, you may set your mind at ease. I have had no cablegram or letter."

" *Oh!*" Val's face became young and her voice her own again. " I thought—I was afraid——"

" I want to hear what explanation you have to give for the way in which you have been deceiving me for all these weeks."

Val was silent.

" I suppose you know what I mean?"

" Yes."

" Well?"

" I wanted pocket-money. It's difficult to get on without any."

" And have you ' got on without any '? Is my memory playing me a trick, or did I slip a shilling into your hand, only a few days ago, and tell you to treat your friend to an ice?"

Val said nothing.

" Did I?"

" Yes, I know, and it was very good of you. But there was the games sub, and—and lots of other things. I don't know if I should really be at Myra Dakin's at all, but, as I am, it seemed sensible to take the chance of earning a little money when I had it."

" Did it not also seem the right course to inform me, who am for the present, your guardian, of your intention?"

" Yes. I meant to tell you, I meant to tell you to-day. I'll show you my calendar with the red mark on it."

Mrs. Wilby made an indescribable sound of impatient disbelief.

" I'm sorry to think that a daughter of Rose Faukner's should do so low and mean and underhand a thing," she said.

" It wasn't!" said Val trembling. " It was just earning money when I hadn't any. Surely there was no harm in that. I worked hard for it. Sammy knows quite a lot of Latin words, and he can say all his declensions without a mistake. His father is pleased with him. I know I ought to have told you. I meant to tell you—— And I saved up some of the money to pay back what I cost you in extras," she added, unconscious of irony.

Mrs. Wilby glanced up sharply.

" Please do not speak in that insincere and insulting way," she said coldly. " How old are you now, Valentine?"

" Nearly sixteen."

" And do you think, seriously, that Mrs. Seyton wanted a girl of sixteen to teach her boy? Was that, do you suppose, her intention when she advertised for a Latin coach?"

" I don't know."

" Valentine, you *do* know. Try to speak sincerely. Did she not object to you on the score of your youth, and change her opinion when she heard you were the daughter of an acquaintance of her school days?"

" Yes, she did," said Val, desperately. " But she's not sorry she did."

" Of course she is not sorry. She knew perfectly well what she was doing, as charitable persons do, and was prepared for the consequences. But she sees the matter differently now."

Val looked up quickly.

" You haven't been to see her?"

" And why should you be so much alarmed lest I should have seen her? Surely it is very natural that I should call upon a woman whom I knew when we were girls together? Your behaviour is extraordinary, Valentine, most extraordinary."

" And I'm not to go there again?" Val was quick

D 503

"SHALL I ASK COOLING FOR A TIN-OPENER?"

and definite, like a grown-up woman, ridiculously, thought Mrs. Wilby, watching her in a queer detached way, like Rose Faukner, leaning across a desk at school, her blue eyes dark with a live anger and resolution, her face white against the dusky tangle of her hair. "You did that, Florence. It's because of you that that happened to me." She almost expected to hear Rose Faukner say it again, in that rapid certain voice, sharp with pain, strong with something in herself that the other girls recognized quite well, though they did not analyse it to themselves. But Rose Faukner was Rose Forrest now, tired, ill, lying in the garden of a nursing home somewhere near Montreal, resting day after day to win her old strength back to her again, and this was only Rose Faukner's girl, a chit of sixteen, powerless to follow whatever her will might be without the consent of her guardian.

"Most certainly you are not. Mrs. Seyton does not wish you to go. When she realized your position, and the importance of your working hard at your lessons, and taking every advantage of being able to attend such a school as Myra Dakin's, she very much regretted having given way to her first impulse, an impulse which seemed so kindly, and which, as, of course, she now sees, was so utterly foolish." Mrs. Wilby paused a moment. "To see a girl sacrifice her chances for greed of money—a *girl!*" she said, in a tone of faint disgust.

" But I didn't. I was second in the form list last week. I can do my prep quite easily in the time set. And I'm not greedy for money." Val said these things listlessly, as if they must be said, but as if she knew they would not be believed.

" Second? Second? Quite!" said Mrs. Wilby. " Second is not exactly the same as first, is it, Val? I do not think your mother would call second and first the same."

She leaned across and patted Val's hand.

" This has all been very unpleasant, dear, and I'm afraid I shall never be able quite to forget that you have deliberately deceived me, but I shall do my best, for your mother's sake."

" Don't forget it," said Val in a strange voice. " If you really think it, go on thinking it. It would be far better."

" I hope you do not intend to show that resentment I don't like in you, Val. You must try to see things from your present guardian's point of view. It is my duty, for the present, to see that you do not waste your opportunities."

" I know. I do see it from your point of view. I tried to tell you, and I was going to tell you to-day."

" Well, we will let that pass just now. Run upstairs quickly, dear, and fetch what you say you have saved. That must not be wasted in ices and sweets. We must put that by for some occasion when you really need money, and my poor little purse is not equal to your demands."

Val fetched her money, deposited in a child's savings-bank, a pillar-box of bright red tin, and put on the table by Mrs. Wilby.

" I'm not sure how much there is in it. About one pound ten, I think," she said. " Shall I ask Cooling for a tin-opener?"

Mrs. Wilby gave a little affected laugh.

" Dear child, no! I think we can trust one another, you and I. See, I will just slip it in here." She lifted the tasselled cover of the table, pulled out a drawer, and put in the money-box. " Nasty stuff! Charity money, I don't like to think of it. But there it is." She rearranged the cover.

" I earned it," said Val. " It was my salary."

" Well, well, dear, I suppose you'll always see it like that. I suppose it's just a question of pride. Now—no more visits to Thornytangle." She laid her warm, plump hand on the little brown one Val held clenched against her side.

" No. I don't suppose I'll go there again."

" Good girl! We quite understand one another, after all, I see. Now run off to your luncheon. I had mine outside to-day, but I told Cooling to set yours in the morning-room, as usual. Give me a kiss, dear."

Val looked in astonishment at the proffered cheek.

To refuse would be absurd—would make it all seem to matter so much more than it did. She gave the kiss, wondering vaguely why Mrs. Wilby wanted it, and feeling unlike herself, like a Val Forrest dressed up in someone else's clothes and stuffed into a shape that wasn't her own, went slowly to where a plate of congealed hash and mottled potato, and another of lukewarm rice embellished with a teaspoonful of treacle, awaited her in the morning-room.

CHAPTER XIII

Val's Luck is Out

Val went to school next morning with something of the wrecked hopeless sensation of the beginning of term, and was met by Pauline and Julie in the highest of high spirits.

" Come along to the gym at once," said they. " Miss Sylvester is trying people for *Twelfth Night*—and she wants you to be Viola."

Instantly Val forgot the problem of how to be her ordinary pleasant schoolgirl self while at The Turret, and raced with the others across the paved court which led to the outbuilding of the gymnasium. Other girls were there: Corinna and Aileen, and a shrewd cheeky little character who was to be Maria, and a big square girl who could deepen her voice in roars of laughter, for Sir Toby, and a dark elegant Upper Fifth Former who was just then speaking one of Olivia's soliloquies. Not to be Val Forrest, decidedly out of love with herself, at all, but Viola, lonely and troubled, brave and gay—it seemed the best thing that could happen just at that moment.

" Hop up to the platform, Val," said Miss Sylvester.
" We'll try you bewildered and swaggering and
frightened and romantic—and we'll have to hurry up
if we're to do all that before prayers. Here's the book."

" I think I know it," said Val.

" I believe you do. Come along—we'll have you
with the ring first. Hurry up, Malvolio——"

Miss Sylvester hurried up all in-between things:
over a poem or play itself there was no rush. No one
wanted Val's scenes to end quickly. Her appearance
helped her: her straight boyish young figure, her
short dark hair, curling in round her ears and the nape
of her neck, and the something a little aloof and for-
lorn in her bearing that had made Miss Sylvester say
during that first lesson " Read Viola!" She liked
Viola; she liked what she said and did; she seemed to
know about her, as if she had seen her; and her words
came naturally, and were easily remembered.

" You'll be the one, I think," said Miss Sylvester,
as the bell rang. " Rehearsals every afternoon at four
—and we must discuss the question of dresses."

" You act well, don't you?" said Corinna, as the
Upper Fifth Olivia consulted Miss Sylvester about
her part. The Fifth generally put a compliment in
the form of a question.

" I don't, you know. I couldn't be anyone else in
Twelfth Night. I couldn't change into Malvolio, as
Pauline does, or into Feste, like Julie. It's queer that

I should have a big part, like Viola's. It makes me feel rather a swindle."

" Why do you do it, then?" snapped Aileen. " Why not leave it to someone who can act?"

" Keep calm, pet," advised Julie. " You'll need all your wits to be a gentleman attending on the Duke. That's the sort of part that takes some doing, especially if you have to say ' Ay, good my lord ', or something of the sort—just enough to be husky over, and no extra words to give you a chance to recover, and show the audience what acting is."

" I am not an attendant on the Duke, as it happens," said Aileen in the tone of elaborate satire. " I am a lady-in-waiting to Olivia, and understudy to Viola."

" Are you *really*?" With quick friendliness and interest Val spun round and looked at Aileen, who was flushed and resentful.

" Yes, I am *really*. Does it astonish you so much?"

" It does!" cried the rest of the Fifth present, with relish.

" Perhaps you'll do it one day, and I'll do it the next," said Val, moved by the instinct to make things right for Aileen which sometimes astonished her by its persistence.

" *Perhaps*," said Aileen, who seemed to have lost faith in the justice of the world. And then the bell rang and the Fifth departed for roll-call and the day's work.

It was a day's work for Val. She was determined to prove that she hadn't slacked that term, and to step from the second to the first place—for a week or two, at any rate. She had come to Myra Dakin's too late to top the final list, for which the total marks gained during the session were counted, and, even had she started with the rest, she doubted if she could have beaten Pauline, who, as top of the form, seemed in her right place. " But I ought to get a fairly decent report," she reflected. " It'll convince Mother that I didn't neglect school work for Sammy's Latin, even if it doesn't convince Mrs. Wilby." And her heart grew a little heavy again, and she felt objectionable and perplexed, as she thought of that lady's patient attitude towards her as a naughty tiresome girl, and her gentle but resolute refusal to be interested in what she liked, or to realize her point of view. " But it won't be for *ever*," she thought. " I must just leave it to time, as Viola did.

> ' O time! thou must untangle this, not I;
> It is too hard a knot for me to untie.' "

With this resolve she went back to The Turret, to find that Mrs. Wilby had placed a few pansies in a small jar on her dressing-table. Full of amazement and contrition, she thanked her guardian, and, determined not to repeat the Thornytangle error, told her that she was probably to act the part of the heroine of *Twelfth Night* at the Fifth Form's end of term entertainment.

" Heroine? " said Mrs. Wilby thoughtfully. " The *heroine*, did you say, dear? "

" Yes, Viola, you know. It's part of the work," she added hurriedly. " There's a lot to learn—or there was. I know it pretty well—it all seems so right: it's easy to remember."

" Your mother learned poetry quickly," said Mrs. Wilby. Val pricked up her ears, for her guardian seldom spoke of the girl Rose Faukner with any of the appreciative admiration with which Miss Ellerton and Mrs. Seyton remembered her, and she would have liked to hear more. But no more came, and the Viola subject was dropped.

Val achieved her purpose, and, for one week, found herself at the top of the Fifth. Then sudden calamity befell her in the shape of algebra. She was not naturally mathematical, but, as she had up till this point been going over ground already covered at her former school, and her general intelligence was quick, Miss Dymchurch had not yet discovered her failing, and when, in the difficult problems at the end of the book, it began to make itself apparent, she could not credit it. Miss Dymchurch's peculiarity was that she could not believe that a sane and decent member of society might be unmathematical. Inability to cope with fairly advanced algebraical problems meant that a girl was

badly taught, or mentally deficient, or a slacker. Val
had been taught all right. Miss Dymchurch was sure
of that, as she had done some of the job herself. Her
general demeanour in school pointed to sanity. One
reason for unsatisfactory work remained—the girl was
growing inattentive and dreamy, her mind was deliberately occupying itself with other things and ob-
stinately refusing to grasp general mathematical prin-
ciples. And one flowery June morning, when everything should have gone as easily as a rose opens out,
she indicated this with some emphasis.

" I don't know what's wrong with you," she said,
slapping down the pile of home exercise books she
had brought in with her and looking accusingly at Val,
as if she, and she alone, were responsible for every
mistake in every one of them. " *Are* you a reasonable
being?"

The Fifth straightened itself and looked interested,
while Val appeared suitably doubtful.

" Are you?" repeated Miss Dymchurch.

" I can't do maths very well."

" Now that's the attitude. You say you can't, and
of course you can't. But you can't say you can't,
because you have proved you can——"

The Fifth began to hold their heads.

" And there is no sort of excuse for work of this
kind."

She dashed open Val's algebra book at the last

home exercise, scored with crosses, exclamations, and question marks in red. Val looked at it with that sinking feeling experienced on such occasions by a girl who is used to doing decent work, while one or two characters who had long ago accepted the position of being below human intelligence, and whose meagre little scrawls of algebra were hardly to be seen for the red decoration of Miss Dymchurch's corrections, regarded her with a sort of amused curiosity, wondering why she seemed to mind so much.

" How long did you spend over it?"

" An hour."

" What sort of an hour? When? After the *Twelfth Night* rehearsal, I suppose?"

" Yes."

" In future do your algebra first. You can't solve problems that require a little brainwork when you're romancing about yourself in the Forest of Arden."

The Fifth noted with enjoyment that Miss Dymchurch thought that Viola was Rosalind. They would have been deeply disappointed in her had she failed to say something of the kind. They knew she could get anyone through any examination in mathematics, and thoroughly appreciated her talk on the subject of accuracy. But she would have seemed all wrong had she distinguished between Arden and Illyria—not their Miss Dymchurch at all.

" I got ten for the last exercise I did after rehearsal," said Val ruefully, as she turned back a page.

" That won't last you for the rest of your mathematical life, my child," said Miss Dymchurch drily.

The Fifth thought it might venture a giggle.

" I know. But I shan't have much of a mathematical life. I can do maths sometimes, but I don't really *see* them."

" That'll help you." Miss Dymchurch scrawled the big R.L. which stood for " returned lesson " at the foot of Val's page. " To-morrow afternoon, at four."

Val grew scarlet. A returned lesson was seldom given in the Fifth and Sixth, where bad work, except on very rare occasions, did not mean slackness. It would be entered on her report, and Mrs. Wilby's comments on her neglect of prep would seem justified.

" I really tried," she said in a trembling voice. " I wasn't thinking about the rehearsal for that hour—and I thought the problem was coming out all right——"

" Look at that—and that——" Miss Dymchurch's contemptuous pencil shot from one howler to another. " No, Val, you have enough sense to see that these mistakes are due to rank carelessness. I know this is your first term, but that is really no excuse. If one new girl can manage the work, another can."

She opened a book at a perfect exercise, neatly finished off with a red " 10/10 ", and put it before Aileen. An extraordinary silence fell upon the Fifth— the silence that, among small girls, might have been a groan. Aileen accepted the book without smugness, shut it, and put it in her desk. The Fifth could find no fault with her demeanour. Nor could they have criticized her reception of Miss Sylvester's request that she should rehearse Viola on the following afternoon, as Val would be wanted elsewhere. There was not a trace of the conceit she had displayed on that tennis evening, and when she was chosen as understudy for the part she coveted. " I suppose people want a bit of good luck to make them really nice," thought Val, noticing the change in her, but too sore to appreciate it.

She did her algebra under the supervision of Miss Dymchurch, who was much more inclined to have mercy on the unmathematical when unencumbered by the presence of a class, and then stole up to the gallery at the back of the hall to watch the progress of the rehearsal. The duel scene was going on, and Aileen was playing her part quite amusingly and well. She was one of the people of whom the audience says— " Who would ever have thought she had it in her?" The less prejudiced members of the cast were saying it to one another now, down in the hall. The others grumbled—" Oh, she can act, there's no doubt of that, but Val doesn't need to act, she just *is* Viola." And Val herself thought rather ruefully, " I don't wonder she was a bit rattled. She's really right—she knows how to be other people and I don't. Viola's just an accident."\ And she wondered if Aileen would play the part one night, and was generous enough to hope she would.

After the rehearsal, Miss Sylvester discussed dresses, and Val went down to the hall to get a drawing of Viola's page costume. She liked the short kilted tunic of soft white stuff, the zouave, and the scarlet fez cap. It would not be a difficult rig-out to contrive, and Julie, who had a sewing-machine, and boasted that she could run up anything, from a handkerchief to an overcoat, had promised to help her. A good thing that the Thornytangle money was stowed away in the pillar-box. It would buy mercerized cotton, and black velvet, and scarlet felt, and a tassel. She was thankful that she had told Mrs. Wilby at once that she was to act in the play. The need of the costume was a fore-gone conclusion—all that must be done now was simply to ask for the money, put by for some such purpose. And yet Val experienced an odd little lurking doubt. She didn't state it even to herself, silently, but she was beginning to feel that Mrs. Wilby didn't like her to have things she liked. She wished the materials for the dress were safely bought.

" I have my lady-in-waiting's costume already,"

Aileen, encouraged by their attention to her acting, told the Fifth. " I'll show it to you to-morrow if you like—it's really rather nice."

" Really rather nice." A few weeks ago it would have been " simply *sweet* ", " quite too dinky ". Aileen was learning the virtues of under-statement— the only sort of description of personal property tolerated at Myra Dakin's. And when, on the next day, she lifted the purple cardboard lid of the dress-box she had lugged to school (Aunt Carol having unsympathetically refused the services of the car), drew out a cloud of tissue paper, and displayed her gown, she had the satisfaction of seeing that the Fifth Formers gathered round her were really impressed. It was made in the most lovely fantastic fashion that might have been worn in Illyria at *Twelfth Night* time, in rich silky stuff that had the sheen of flame, and it was the colour of flame. Val thought she had never seen anything more beautiful. " I didn't know dress-makers made things like that," she said, in an awed voice, touching it very gently, as if it might crumble away into ashes. " It's like a sycamore tree in Sep-tember. No, that's too pale—daffodils—marigolds—sunset—no, fire. You'll feel on fire when you wear it, Aileen."

" I hope not," laughed Aileen, speaking directly to Val for almost the first time since the tennis with the Fifth. " If this dress were burnt I don't suppose my people would rise to another quite like it."

" I should think not," sighed the Fifth, lost in the wonder of it, seeing themselves grown up, marvellously beautiful, and going to dances in lovely shimmery frocks on which no expense had been spared. Pauline alone seemed unimpressed.

" I thought Olivia's court was in mourning," she said.

" Feste is, anyway," said Julie, who was exercising her wits in the evenings on magpie motley of black and white.

" There's no authority for it in the play," said Aileen loftily.

" It's so obvious that there's no need to say it," returned Pauline. " And it *does* say that Olivia hates yellow. That's the point of Malvolio's yellow stockings."

The Fifth looked rather doubtfully from the dress to Pauline's handsome, rather scoffing face. For once they thought her carping rather than clever, but, quite uninfluenced by their opinion, she continued to express her own.

" Imagine poor old Olivia in black velveteen at a few shillings a yard and her attendant got up like *that*," she said.

" But royal ladies aren't always the best dressed," reflected Julie. " Haven't you ever read about how economical they are, and what an example, and how the younger children wear things the big ones have grown out of, suffering just like the rest of us?"

"Olivia's dress is being made out of a black velveteen her mother once wore in the evening," said Val. " There used to be lots of stuff in a skirt then, and she says it's coming out all right."

" There you are! Noble to the backbone—all in keeping," said Julie in triumph.

" It may be like that in real life, but it isn't on the stage," asserted Pauline, unmoved. " The audience must know at once which is *the* person—and before she begins to speak they know it by her clothes. Go to any London theatre and you'll see."

This being quite beyond the present power of the Fifth, they looked a little impressed.

" Of course it is a perfectly glorious dress," went on Pauline. " The sort of thing Lady Macbeth and Goneril wear, though why they should bag all the splendid colours I don't know. Why shouldn't Cordelia have a sort of glow about her, and her hair in a jewelled net, instead of being so wishy-washy bread-and-milkish, like a portrait of a fair maid given away with the grocery at Christmas."

" And why shouldn't a maid of honour, if you want to be unconventional?" put in Julie, recognizing that Pauline was off on a favourite topic. " Besides, Aileen may understudy Viola, and then the dress will come in nicely."

"What for?   Being washed up wet from a wreck?" inquired Pauline sardonically.

The Fifth gave it up, all but Val.

"At the end Orsino asks Viola to change into woman's weeds," she said.   "She might manage it in time for the audience to have a look at her."

"But what has Viola got to do with it?" demanded Pauline, swinging round and taking Val's arm.   "You're Viola, aren't you?   Dymmer hasn't had you fired from the play because you couldn't do your algebra?"

"No."

"Well!"

Going back to The Turret, Val wondered what sort of page's dress Aileen would have, were she to play Viola on one of the two nights for which the entertainment was to run.   She would hardly consent to wear the outfit which, Val thought ruefully, would, even with the help of Julie, be at best but passable.   But however it might turn out, it must be made at once. Mrs. Wilby had called at Lyncote that afternoon. She liked visiting the Ellertons, and might be in a really good humour, ready to sympathize with, even perhaps to show active interest in, the difficulties of buying stuff, and using it in the best way.   Val went straight into the snuggery, guessing that she would be arranging flowers from the Lyncote garden there. But before she had time to ask for the money, Mrs. Wilby spoke.

" Val, I am sorry to hear that, after our little heart-to-heart talk a few weeks ago, you are still wasting your time in school."

Val opened her eyes. The misfortune of the algebra had sent her down a place or two, but this week she was pulling up, and Miss Dymchurch had awarded an eight out of ten, with the resigned comment that she supposed she was gradually coming to her senses. She had hated the returned lesson, and was ashamed of it—but she knew it wasn't due to slacking, and she knew somehow that Miss Dymchurch, in spite of her sharp tongue, wouldn't formally complain of a lesson, over which full time had been spent, to her guardian or to the head mistress. The R.L. would appear on her final report, but not till then.

" I'm not," she said. " I came down over some algebra I didn't understand. That's all."

" ' That's all.' Dear, I do wish you would not be so glib and easy over your own failures and shortcomings. I'm afraid that you won't improve as long as you see yourself as so entirely perfect a person."

" I don't. I can't do maths easily—I made a fearful mess of one exercise. I've cleared it up a bit this week. That's all. I mean, that explains it."

" Not quite. I hear that you are rehearsing every evening for a prominent part in some play that is being done in school."

" Three times a week. *Twelfth Night*. Don't you

remember? I told you when we began," said Val
anxiously. " I'm Viola—and I was going to ask you
this evening for money to buy stuff for the costume."

" Money, dear? Costume?"

" Yes. The rest of the Thornytangle money, you
know."

" Oh yes. I should have thought you would hardly
care to allude to that again. I could hardly see my way
to letting you waste your money, when you have so
little, in dressing yourself up in stage finery. But of
course you must withdraw from this play."

The safe snuggery seemed to topple like a Cubist
picture. Val gasped.

" Oh, Mrs. Wilby! Oh, *why?* You don't mean it—
you can't! It's such fun. It's such an honour. I do
love doing it so. I'm not wasting my time, honestly,
I'm not. Ask anybody; if they say I am I'll give up
the play without another word."

" If you think of the remarks made to you by your
form mistress the other day before the entire class, you
will perhaps withdraw your suggestion that I should
' ask anybody '," said Mrs. Wilby coldly. " I shall,
of course, write to your head mistress. She knows
your circumstances, and I think she will understand."

" Mother would love me to be in it," stammered
Val, hoping that she was not going to cry.

" Fortunately you are not now in a position to make

a scene and compel your mother to give you luxuries she cannot afford."

It was useless. Useless to point out that the material would cost only a few shillings; useless to remind Mrs. Wilby of the money in the toy bank, to try to prove that the rehearsals did not waste time, that her mother would have " loved her to be in it ". She saw that Mrs. Wilby had resolved that she should not play the part, and, with a stoicism Pauline might have envied, she accepted the situation.

" All right," she said, in a queer, detached, grown-up voice. " Shall I tell Miss Sylvester myself—or will Miss Beauchamp do it?"

" I have written to Miss Beauchamp. If you are a sensible girl—as your mother's daughter should be—you will not air your grievances in public. The managers of this play seem very much delighted with little Nina's rendering of the part—the child is, of course, a born actress. In fact, dear, your withdrawal may save you from the rather humiliating experience of being asked to withdraw. You must try to look at it in that light, and any disappointment you may feel will soon vanish."

Val didn't look at it in that light, or in any light at all. Once she was up in her room her stoicism disappeared. She hated people to cry, but cry she did, as stormily as a child who has lost its weekly money or been told that it can't go to the party. And, like a child, she couldn't see beyond her disappointment. For that evening she felt it would always be like that, always what made her happy would be lopped off, and never would she be the ordinary Val Forrest, enjoying people and things naturally as they came along, never again.

CHAPTER XIV

A Surprise for Aileen

Next morning Val felt better. She did not tell the Fifth generally what had happened—not because she followed anyone's good advice, but simply because for some reason she didn't want to. She was never one to crave or care very much for public sympathy, public indignation on her behalf. But she did tell Pauline. And Pauline, generally remarkable for contained behaviour, lost her temper with satisfactory vigour and completeness.

"It's absolute rot!" she declared. "I don't know anything about Mrs. Wilby. I don't know why on earth she should force you to throw up Viola. I don't know why you suddenly gave up teaching Sammy Seyton, when you could stand him quite well and wanted pocket-money. I suppose her mind worked along the same lines both times."

"I suppose so. Slacking over school work."

"My——" Pauline really did not know what ejaculation met the case, so left it at that. "I just wish she could *see* a slacker, one with her heart in it—or even a middling one, like most people." She paused. "Of course she's been deluded," she went on in a calmer voice. "She's been deluded by that ridiculous pet with the ringlets."

Val stared.

"Oh, Paul, I don't think so!"

"All right. Listen. Doesn't she visit the Ellertons?"

"Yes, but——"

"Don't but. Didn't you tell Aileen Ellerton that you were coaching Sammy Seyton?"

"Yes. I had to explain why I couldn't come out to Lyncote as often as she asked me."

"Good. A mistake, of course; you should have told me and me alone. Didn't you say that Mrs. Wilby tackled you about it just as you were on the verge of telling her?"

"Yes, but——"

"And how do you suppose she knew? Hadn't she just come from Lyncote?"

"I believe she had, but, Paul, I don't think I asked Aileen to keep it secret. It wasn't secret—I meant to tell it myself, you see——"

"And about this play business. D'you suppose Aileen got that dress with a view to being a maid-of-honour? Not a bit, it's to shine out as Viola in the pavan or whatever they're dancing at the end. She'd made up her mind to have the part, and she has it. She'd

recite all that Dymchurch harangue with gusto—it's
not a bit the same thing when you don't know that
Dymmer really goes a little mad while teaching class
maths—and her mother, who's probably the same
sort, would dish it up to your Mrs. Wilby, who'd
promptly get the wind up over her duty by you and
letting you waste your time and the rest of it. A mistake, of course, but you can't expect her to see your
true interests as your mother would—and even mothers
are sometimes rather too susceptible to rumours about
what goes on in school——"

Pauline broke off, looking reminiscent.

"Oh, well. I don't know," sighed Val. "It's done
now, anyway. I'm going to find a four-leaved clover
or a bit of white heather or make a pilgrimage to a
wishing well this summer. I'm getting tired of my
luck—it's too badly out."

"All right. Let's make an excursion to Rookmere
one Saturday—Corinna and Julie and you and I, and
organize a search-party for luck. There's a fairy spring
near the lake—a drink from that might help—and
we'll find the clover too."

"Perhaps one oughtn't to mix luck. I must do the
right thing if I get a chance. It's really important."

"Well, I've one good piece of news for you. I meant
to tell you first thing this morning, but the horrible
unfairness of this Viola business put it out of my
head. My people have seen your mother, and she's

a lot better, and was tremendously pleased to hear about you."

" Oh, Pauline!" Relief lightened Val's heart, and for the moment she forgot her disappointment.

" They were evidently much charmed," said Pauline, who believed in telling people she liked things that would please them. " I gather they spent a week-end in talking about you. Your letters were growing a bit scrappy, your mother said—she supposed you were fairly overwhelmed with occupations at school."

" She wasn't supposed to have letters, you know," said Val. " I was just allowed to write small ones, with everything exciting left out."

" Who said so?"

" Mrs. Wilby. It was in the letter from old Mr. Hunniker."

" Oh. Then you haven't been able to tell anyone your troubles?"

" Except you, some of them." Val laughed. " I feel better now," she said. " I could almost believe I was going to be Viola after all."

" You may," said Pauline. " Don't forget the words. Something will happen, and you'll romp home as heroine after all."

It sounded convincing, this optimism from Pauline, who, in theory at any rate, was inclined to regard life as a black business. But nothing immediately justified it. Miss Beauchamp sent for Val and talked to her

about her work. " Your present guardian is naturally
anxious for you to make the most of your opportunities," she said. " I must say you seem to be doing
pretty well—but you mustn't be too easily pleased
with yourself. Always, in the allotted time, give all
your energy to the matter in hand—work to the very
top of your capacity." Val, who naturally tackled
things with vigour, promised to do what she generally
did, and the interview between head mistress and girl,
both slightly puzzled as to what it was all about, came
to an end. Miss Dymchurch, Val gathered, had been
" spoken to " on the subject of her algebra, with the
result that Miss Dymchurch stoutly refused to
acknowledge that she was slack or unmathematical,
and ministered to her understanding with the tender
solicitude a sympathetic nurse shows a suffering
patient, greatly to the entertainment of the Fifth.
Miss Sylvester made no comment on Val's withdrawal from the play: in fact, at the end of a couple of
days, Val began to wonder if she had ever been in it.
Then Aileen, who, though Val had not been in the
mood to notice them, had recently shown signs of
emerging from ill humour, ran after her as she left
morning school and caught her up not far from the
gate.

" I'm glad *you* like my dress so much," she said
confidentially, as if she had never thought of " hating "
Val. " Evidently I'm to be Viola on one night after all.

Isn't it jolly? I'm so glad about it. I shan't wear the
dress for the sea-beach, of course, any old dark wrap
will do for that, but it'll be gorgeous for the pavan
at the end. And what I wanted to say just now was that
I'll lend it to you for your night—we're about the same
size, and it'll fit you beautifully, and a dark-haired
person will look as nice in it as a fair one——"

She broke off, perhaps feeling that Val was unre-
sponsive.

"Are you pleased?" she said. "You'd like it,
wouldn't you, Val? You do think it's a pretty dress,
don't you?"

"I think it's perfectly lovely. But what's the use
of offering it to me, when I'm out of the play?"

Aileen stared.

"Out of it?"

"Yes. Didn't you know? I thought you did."

"But why?"

Val suddenly felt savage. The queer protective
instinct for Aileen deserted her; she thought her stupid
as well as spoilt, and saw no generosity in an offer
which, as its maker very likely knew, could not be
accepted. Although she had not at once believed
Pauline's suggestions as to the mischief-making of
Aileen, they had remained in her mind, and she could
not but feel that in the " I hate you " mood a good deal
of harm might be done, however sorry for it the doer
might afterwards be.

" Mrs. Wilby has the idea I'm slacking," she said shortly. " Someone reported that scene with Dymmer in full, you see. Less *Twelfth Night* and more algebra is the idea, I suppose."

Aileen looked red and distressed.

" But, Val, Miss Dymchurch likes you. She didn't really want you to be turned out of the play."

" Of course she didn't," snapped Val. " And I wasn't turned out, you know. I wasn't allowed to be in."

" Oh—I'm sorry about it, Val. I'm sorry for you, really I am."

" Thanks."

They had come to the corner where the station road branched from that leading to The Turret. Without another word, Val strode off, while Aileen stared after her, amazed. Val had never been like that before, never. She couldn't understand it at all.

CHAPTER XV

An Unlooked-for Disaster

As after the break with the Seytons and Thorny-tangle, Val found a little consolatory offering from Mrs. Wilby on her dressing-table, this time in the form of two roses. But she could not feel softened and ashamed, as she had done on the previous occasion. " Thank you " suddenly seemed an impossibly difficult phrase. " I ought to have told her before about the Latin," she thought. " But this Viola thing is unfair right through. What's the good of taking away what I liked so much, and then giving me roses, like a friend? People who queer your pitch should be consistent." She stared impatiently at the roses—examples of the one rose in the world which isn't a success, pinkish red, mottled with white like a sort of soap, never reaching the right rose's moment of absolute perfection in fragrance and shape, but over-blown when full-blown, and always smelling a little of decay. " I'm glad they're not the heavenly kind," she reflected. " I suppose I must say thank you very much for them." But she didn't, and, oddly, Mrs.

Wilby did not allude to them, or reprove her for ingratitude and impoliteness.

Although she was an only child, Val never had had things all her own way. Her father and mother, in their fear lest she should be pampered and objectionable, had seen to it that she played and worked a great deal with other children, and that she shared what she had with them. Small jealousies and selfishnesses had been treated with a scornful little laugh or comment, as if they simply weren't worth any further consideration, and in consequence Val had really had rather less than her fair share of the ordinary weakness of the ordinary little girl. She had enough spirit to hold her own, but she did it with independence, so marked had been the discouragement such remarks as " It isn't fair ", " I shan't play ", " I'll pay her out ", " I'll tell mother ", always met with. She was quite astonished at the feelings which the Fifth at first displayed when they finally realized that she had dropped out of *Twelfth Night*, and that Aileen had taken her place for good, and surprise was succeeded by alarm when she saw the lengths to which they were prepared to go in the way of public demonstration.

" Oh, but *don't*," she said when Julie, of all people, hinted at these. " It would seem like jealousy, and people are always talking about petty little jealousies in girls' schools."

" ' People are always talking!' " said Pauline with a
snort. " Girls' schools, forsooth——"

Val gazed at her.

" Well—don't you think it's true?"

" True, oh yes, it's true, because it's true of everywhere. Ask an actress—ask a cabinet minister—ask
a man in an office—ask a church worker——"

" Ask them all yourself, Paul," said Julie, " and tell
us the answers if you like."

" I would if there were any need to," said Pauline.
" But there isn't. I know."

" The understanding eye," said Julie. " Send up
a sample of your handwriting to Paul and get your
character, if you'd like it."

" You wouldn't," said Pauline unmoved. " But I
do know it, anyhow. There's nothing in knowing it.
It's like having an ear for music—only it's an ear for
the savage breast instead."

Julie lifted Pauline's dark side lock, and inspected
her particularly small and well-shaped ear.

" Quite normal," she said. " In fact, rather nice.
A pity it should be fashionable to cover up *one* of your
good points, Paul."

Pauline smoothed down her hair.

" To go back to the original topic," she said,
" this Aileen-Val-Viola business, and the sentiments it arouses, are no more petty than —
than——"

"The Battle of Waterloo?" suggested Corinna hopefully.

"Entirely useless as a parallel," said Pauline. "I'll think it over and let you know later. Meanwhile you may all express your petty sentiments with every confidence in the equal pettiness of your fellow-creatures."

"Have a twopenny fancy, Paul," said Julie, producing a bag. "And it'll need all your attention— nothing doing for several minutes, but when your tooth suddenly gets through almost more than enough."

"Thank you." And Pauline meditatively bit into the big squirled chocolate, while Val thought, as she often did, how much she liked the Fifth, and, as she had done for a few days, what particularly hard luck it was that she shouldn't be able to act with them. But, though honestly irritated with her, she did not work up any personal grudge against Aileen, and in a few days the violence of the sentiments of the Fifth subsided, and without any particular comment they accepted the new Viola. Only Pauline, polite, showing neither friendliness nor hostility, remained guarded.

Viola's clothes continued to interest the Fifth. The flame-coloured garment to be put on for the pavan was followed by a page's dress which made Becky Ellicott, playing the part of Sebastian, look at first delighted, then doubtful. It was heartening to think that her own costume, modelled on the same lines, might be equally effective, daunting to realize that family skill—" Why, dear, I'll run it up for you in half an hour on my machine "—might not succeed in making it so. All the materials were of the very best obtainable: the sword-belt, in subdued and yet glowing tangle of colour, was beautiful to look at closely, held in the hand, and yet effective from the distance of the auditorium: the cut and finish of the short pleated tunic and the jaunty zouave, so often disregarded by the *costumière* of the amateur theatrical society, were as perfect as a famous firm could make them. Aileen was charming in the dress, which gave her the slight swagger she needed, especially in the playing of the first scene in Olivia's house.

" It's lovely, Aileen," said Becky. " I only hope I'll look a quarter as nice—nice enough for Sebastian really to be mistaken for Cesario."

" That's a problem," said Julie.

" Easy enough," said Pauline. " Cesario presumably had his second best uniform on, running down into Illyria to do the shopping in the morning, when so much trouble arose."

For an instant Aileen appeared to consider giving Pauline one of the famous glances, but decided to ignore her, and displayed to the Fifth the wrap in which Viola traditionally makes her first appearance on the stage after the rescue from the split ship. The Fifth, who had visualized the " any old thing "

suggested by the circumstances, gasped with pleasure
when they saw the folds of deep and cloudy blue, and
the splendid colours and gleam of gold in the arabesque
design of the border.

" If I were you I should want to wear these lovely
things all the time, Aileen," said Julie. " I couldn't
be an ordinary Myra Dakin again after having had
them on—I couldn't."

" Try on the cloak." Aileen turned to Val, who
stood looking on, fascinated.

Val flushed a bit, and shook her head, with a friendly
little smile. Her disappointment was wearing less
sharp—to pretend again to be Viola would bring it
back.

" *Come* along." Aileen flung the wrap over Val's
shoulders, and drew it round her chin. It fell into its
own perfect folds down along her tall young figure.
A bit of the gleaming border lay against her cheek
and short dark hair: her eyes, a little distressed, were
suddenly deepened in colour by the lovely blue. The
girls looked at her.

" Why, violet eyes don't mean that at all!" said
Pauline, with apparent irrelevance. " I always thought
they meant the kind you buy in shops, violets in shops,
and must be a fake, for no eyes are purple like that, or
ought to be. They don't. They mean those grey
wood violets, of *course*. I never thought of it. Then
there *are* violet eyes, and I said in my last comp but

one about heroines in fiction that there *weren't*, and Miss Sylvester didn't correct it."

"Add a footnote and point it out," said Julie. "You look like a princess, Val, one of the genuine old fairy-tale kind, you know."

Aileen gently removed the wrap from Val's shoulders.

"I shall wear it at rehearsal to-day," she said. "I must get used to waddling about in the old thing. There's such a lot of it."

"Only about sixty lines to waddle in, though," said Julie. "You can't do much in that time, even if you give your whole mind to it."

Miss Sylvester agreed, however, that it might be a good plan to become accustomed to the management of drapery. Encouraged by the admiration of the girls, and that sense of "*Now* we're coming to the real thing" which the first appearance of the right costume awakes in the company, Aileen changed into her page's dress for the third scene, and into the flame-coloured "woman's weeds", still first favourite, for the end of the last act. Applause was unstinted, and, though it was still some weeks from the end of term, Aileen continued to come to rehearsals arrayed as if for the final performance of the play.

"I don't know if I should change *every* time, Aileen," said Miss Sylvester one Friday.

"But you said——"

" I know, but I think you *are* used to it now. It would be such a pity if those lovely things of yours were damaged in any way before the night. It's often rather dusty on this platform by the evenings, and first freshness goes rather quickly——"

> " Women are as roses, whose fair flower
> Being once displayed, doth fall that very hour,"

sighed Julie.

" And the fair flower of carnival clothes is as bad," said Miss Sylvester.

" I like to *be* Viola, though. I like to be her all through." Aileen looked rapt.

" Of course. And it's good not to feel awkward in her rig-out—but on the other hand being too much accustomed to it may make you stale. People who can't act very well sometimes are wrought up to do wonderfully by the mere shock of finding themselves in unfamiliar clothes," said Miss Sylvester.

Pauline looked thoughtful, but Miss Sylvester noticed it in time.

" Hurry up! Olivia, quick, quick! Priest—priest— where *is* that priest? Gone into the garden because he hasn't anything to say? What rubbish—*fetch* him, Corinna, and tell him to wait behind after the re-hearsal for a word with me. Top speed, now! Sebastian! Oh, you're there, are you? That's all right. Now then—' This is the air; that is the glorious sun;

This pearl she gave me, I do feel't and see't,' " Miss
Sylvester's voice, with the suddenness which had
ceased to astonish the Fifth, slid from its staccato
energizing to the slow movement of Sebastian's
wonder, and Becky, far happier when belabouring Sir
Andrew than when thinking over Olivia's strange
kindness, tried uneasily to imitate. The rehearsal had
begun.

Val watched for a little, went down to the prep
room and did algebra for an hour, played half a set of
tennis with some eager juniors who wanted a fourth.
When she returned to the gym, by way of the flight
of stairs from the garden and the short passage leading
past a couple of dressing-rooms, the *Twelfth Night*
company had gone.

Disappointed, she searched the little rooms. Aileen
must still be in school. The flame-coloured dress lay
over the back of a chair, and a school hat hung on one
of the pegs. Probably she would be working off
arrears for Miss Dymchurch or Miss Sylvester somewhere. She was quite a clever girl and prepared her
work conscientiously if she happened to be there when
it was given out—but she could not or would not
grasp the regulation which ordained that, if absent
from a class for a single day, a girl must on her return
find out the prep for the next one, and do it, if possible.
Julie declared that if the parting of her hair didn't
come straight Aileen thought she was ill, and certainly

she was rather often absent and rather often detained
for neglected prep in consequence. Thinking back,
Val remembered that she hadn't been at the last
geometry lesson.

"It'll be Dymmer," she said to herself. "Wonder
how long she'll keep her. Wonder if it's worth waiting."

She was in the mood for companionship, and Aileen
had been nice about that cloak. She remembered the
colour and feel of it, and, with a little pang of pleasure,
the instant admiration of the girls when she put it
on. Only Julie had really *said* anything—but she must
have looked quite decent. What had made Pauline
have that bright idea, that very bright idea, about
grey violets? She knelt on a chair and looked in the
small square of glass, apparently designed, as most
school mirrors seem to be, with the express intention
of acting as a check to vanity. In this one a slight crack
ran over the surface, badly damaging the reflection
of the eyes about which their owner felt a new curiosity.
Val was tickled, and grinned to herself.

"No hope," she thought. "I'm not even to have a
quiet few minutes admiring my beauty. I may as well
get back to The Turret."

Back she got, and spent a rather trying week-end,
Mrs. Wilby being in what she called the "hinting
mood". It was lightened by the probability of a
long picnic at Rookmere with Pauline and company
on the following Saturday. As usual, Val was glad to

return to Myra Dakin's on Monday. She was at
school early, and went at once to the gym, where a
few of the *Twelfth Night* girls often had an impromptu
rehearsal before the bell rang for prayers.

There was no one on the platform, but excited
voices from the small dressing-room told her that some
of the players had arrived. She ran across the big
gym, into the passage, and there, before an open door,
stopped short, in sudden dismay.

Corinna was there, and Pauline, and Julie, and
Becky, and Rhoda Morrison, the unfortunate priest,
who had been so much impressed by Miss Sylvester's
" word " after the performance, that she had come to
school early to stand about on the stage or say her
eight lines or run errands for the others or do anything that might be required of her. Aileen was there,
too, pink and ruffled, as she had been on the morning
of the hat episode, at the beginning of term. And
indeed she had good reason to be perturbed. The
lovely flame-coloured dress still hung over the chair.
As she saw Val standing in the doorway she snatched
it up and held it out, and there, across the skirt and one
shoulder, were the marks of a pair of hands—hands
that had worked hard sweeping, and dusting, and
polishing, and black-leading, and, making everything
bright and clean, had acquired too much of the grime
they had removed to touch a light gay fabric without
leaving their very definite imprint.

" Oh!" Val's distress was as genuine as if the mishap had been hers. She could not bear to see a lovely thing spoiled.

" Don't worry too much till you've seen it from a distance, Aileen," said Paul, who evidently was very sorry too. " Perhaps it won't show much in artificial light. Just look at what they wear in pantomimes in the provinces sometimes, and the effect is quite good."

" This isn't a pantomime in the provinces," burst out Aileen. " And this dress wasn't meant for an effect which should be quite good. It was meant for a glorious effect, and so it should have been, perfectly glorious, and now it's utterly ruined."

For once Pauline was taken aback, but she recovered.

" It isn't really," she said. " Perhaps Orsino'll be able to wangle himself about in the pavan so that it'll be hidden—the marked bits, anyway. I'll ask him. I'm very, very sorry—it's a shame," she added.

" It *is* a shame. I only hope Miss Beauchamp'll insist that Hobbins discovers which of the charwomen did it. She ought to be put in prison. And Hobbins ought to be punished, too. I wonder what he thinks he's here for! You couldn't call him a caretaker, whatever he is."

" Oh, Aileen!" cried Val. " Did you forget to pack your frock—did you leave it in school?"

The others, faces gloomy with sympathy, turned to give her a glance of greeting. For a minute no one said anything. Her question had brought the situation again before them, as questions of a new-comer often do. Saturday had been the day of the big special monthly cleaning, when extra casual labour was engaged, and the girls were warned to leave no property lying about. If they chose to do so, Miss Beauchamp had said, they must accept the sole responsibility of loss or damage. Mistresses and captains would see that the belongings of absentees were safely stowed away: girls who were present must look after their own.

" It was the big clean," said Corinna. " They won't know who did it."

" And if they did, they couldn't complain." No one spoke, but it almost said itself in the silence in which they looked at Aileen and her dress.

" But, Aileen!" exclaimed Val. " D'you mean to say you didn't wait on Friday to make up maths or English? After the rehearsal?"

" Of course I didn't wait. Why should I? I packed my suit-case at once. I had an extra tennis frock in it: that was why it seemed ordinarily full when I had put the other dresses in, and I didn't realize that I had left out this one, the best of all."

" But your hat?" Val looked towards the peg where the straw hat bound with the Myra Dakin colours had hung. It was still there, but it now seemed astonishingly battered and shabby.

" *That* isn't my hat," said Aileen with dignity.

" Why, Val!" cried Julie. " D'you mean to say that you don't yet know Myrtle Brown?"

Val bit her lip. Of course she knew Myrtle Brown —the hat of an old girl, who, having printed her name three times in its lining, had left it in school when her school days were over, never guessing that it would usurp her personality for itself. It was not given away or sent away or thrown away: it hung about the outer gym dressing-room with the strange endurance sometimes displayed by a fly in winter time. In the downstairs cloakroom it would have been trampled into shreds: here it seemed to lead a charmed life. Everyone in the upper school, changing into her tunic, had at some time knocked down Myrtle Brown, and, with suitable comment, replaced her on her peg. A poem about her had appeared in the school magazine. By what unlucky chance could Val's memory have stood by when she looked in the cloakroom and let her fail to recognize Myrtle Brown?

" What's wrong, Val?" said Julie.

" Why, I was thinking what bad luck it was. I actually came up here on Friday night to find someone to talk to, and saw Aileen's dress lying here, and thought she must be still in school. Dymmer, I thought —and I knew it wouldn't be much good waiting——"

Everyone looked at Val.

" Do you mean to say you saw my dress here and didn't put it away for me!" Aileen was almost breathless.

" I do, worse luck! I thought you must be coming back. If *only* I'd known—the dress might never have been spoiled."

" *Known!*" Aileen was almost beside herself. " Could anything else have made you know—when we had all gone, hats away, and everything—and you saw my poor dress lying there, and wouldn't do anything to protect it!"

" But, Aileen, I thought—Myrtle Brown was there, you know."

" Myrtle Brown!" Aileen glanced at the old hat. And indeed, in the clear light of morning, it did seem impossible for anyone to have mistaken it for a school sailor in current use, especially one belonging to a girl who was always spick and span.

" It was frightfully stupid of me," said Val, her colour heightened, her eyes full of distress.

" Stupid! If it were only stupid! It was *mean*— I shouldn't have thought you'd be so mean, Val."

Aileen's voice trembled, and it seemed as if she were going to burst into tears. As a matter of fact, she knew that she had said more than she meant, and more than she could bear to say to Val, whom she really liked. But she had never been taught to control the

bad old instinct all human beings share, the instinct
to find a scapegoat for personal misfortune for which
one is personally responsible. Anger flashed up in
Val, but before she had time to speak, Pauline inter-
vened.

"Don't say another word, Aileen," she said, "or
you'll be pretty sorry for it—and if you aren't, we'll
rather soon make you."

Aileen choked down a sob, and glanced round the
group, which only a few moments ago, had been in
real sympathy with her. But now all that was changed.
Pauline, who had grown very white, looked hard and
keen and rather terrible; Corinna was trembling a
little, and her face was distressed, and a bit disgusted;
Julie was perfectly solemn, and, in a way, seemed
hard as Pauline. Their sudden and complete withdrawal was more than Aileen could stand.

"It's a shame!" she cried. "It isn't fair! You
always take Val Forrest's part—no one cares what
happens to me, and now my dress is spoilt, and no
one cares, and no one will help me to do a thing, not
a thing."

Pauline stepped forward and lifted the dress from
Aileen's lap, where it was in danger of further damage
from the tears that began to fall. She was very angry,
but she couldn't let good material go to waste like that.

"If only it had been Paul!" thought Val miserably.
"She'd have recognized Myrtle Brown at once, and

realized that Aileen had gone, and locked up the dress. She——"

The bell clanged, and, tidying up their emotions as speedily as they could, the greenroom group joined the rest of the Fifth standing in their line for prayers.

CHAPTER XVI

A Perfect Day and Its Ending

Corinna and Pauline were both full of the scheme of a day's camping at Rookmere, and Pauline made sure that it should not be thwarted at the outset by an obdurate keeper. She wrote to the owner of the place, a Mr. Seton Hayling, and received permission to trespass. " Keepers are always vigilant on Saturdays," she said, producing her pass, and unfolding it before the admiring eyes of the others. " But with this we may go where we will. No one will interfere with us."

" I hope I'll be able to come," sighed Val. " I wish I could have secured my good luck token first."

" You mustn't do that. That's the aim of the excursion," said Pauline. " You'll be able to look back on this Rookmere day and say—From the hour I drank from the fairy pool or walked the fairy path, or whatever you do, my luck changed, and everything now goes so well that I'd like a misfortune or two by the way of variety."

Val laughed.

" Surely no one in the world could ever say that, Paul."

" What are you going to wish for, Val?" Corinna wanted to know. " To be Viola after all, or for your mother to come home?"

" I mustn't tell my wish," said Val. And as she said it she knew that her wish was a negative one. She wanted her mother to come back; she wanted to earn pocket-money as she had done at Thornytangle; she wanted to be in the play again. But most of all she wanted not to live at The Turret. " If only Mrs. Wilby would send me away," she thought. " If only I needn't live with her—how free I should feel! How right everything would come—how easy it would all be again!"

Then she heard Aileen speak to Julie, and listened, indifferently.

" Are you going to picnic at Rookmere? Why, that's quite near Lyncote, near my home. What fun it would be if I came with you?"

Julie looked doubtful. Since the *Twelfth Night* rehearsals, when she had got to know Aileen better, she had become more tolerant of her, but this was Pauline's outing, and Pauline's attitude towards the " mother's pet ", as she persistently described her, was pretty well defined.

" Would it?" she said.

" Yes. I'd love it. I'll bring a lobster salad and

raspberries from the garden—our raspberries are
specially good this year—and cream, and meringues.
I wish I could bring ices, but I suppose there's no
way of carrying them. I suppose it would be impossible and out of the question to get the refrigerator
to the camping-place."

" As impossible as most people find it to butt into
a party when they aren't asked," said Pauline, in a
voice which suggested the properties of the contrivance
in question.

Aileen turned pink, and assumed the haughty and
outraged expression which had once been directed
towards the entire Fifth, and was now generally re-
served for Pauline.

" You're exceedingly rude," she said, and stalked
off. The others looked after her.

" Which was my intention," said Pauline amiably.

" Those viands would have been jolly nice, all the
same," said Julie, in a dreamy and rather regretful
tone. " Buns and lemonade and the cheapest sort of
meat pie will be our stunt, I suppose."

" Campers are always content with hard fare,
though," said Corinna, looking as if she could break
the rule for once with extreme ease. " Don't you remember—

> ' Bed in the bush with stars to see,
> Bread I dip in the river.' "

" I shan't dip my bread in the river for anyone,"

said Julie irritably. "Why should you have the sort of stuff to eat that you used to get when sent to bed for the day, just because you're out of doors enjoying yourself?"

"Well, if you want to sell your soul for lobster, do it," said Pauline largely. "But don't do it with us at Rookmere. This is Val's and my show, and we've asked you two because we quite like you. Aileen Ellerton we don't want to know just now, and, if she trundled a whole canteen-wagon of lobsters to the picnic place, our opinion would remain totally unchanged."

"All right, Paul, don't get rattled. But you're prejudiced. There's nothing really wrong with the girl," said Julie. "Since she did her hair properly she looks quite decent; she really acts jolly well; and she doesn't *always* lose her temper at tennis, and elsewhere."

"M-m-m!" was Pauline's comment, with all the expressiveness it is possible to put into sounds that aren't words. Julie said no more of the delicacies lost, and the four arranged their meeting-place for Saturday with no further thought of the rejection of the self-suggested guest. It occurred to Val later in the day, that, if Pauline's theories were correct, Mrs. Wilby might get to know of the picnic through the Ellertons. "She might forbid me to go," she thought. "She might refuse to believe that we have a permit, or say it would be a waste of time." But nothing of the sort happened. At breakfast on Saturday Mrs. Wilby asked in a tone of gentle resignation, as if prepared for the worst, " And what are your plans for to-day?" and, after Val's tremulous reply—" I'm picnicking with some of the girls," she said no more. However, Val left early and ran to the meeting-place, fearful lest, at the last moment, she should be deprived of the joy of a perfect July day in as perfect a place as Rookmere.

Pauline was there, a little before time, and she at once handed Val a basket of sandwiches and cake, with a blue mug tied to its handle.

" Carry that," she commanded. " That's your burden." She had another mug-adorned basket for herself, as well as a kettle. Nothing had been said on the subject, but she guessed that Val wouldn't be able to bring anything to the picnic, and wasn't going to have any palaver about it before Julie and Corinna. There was Val's share and contribution, and, for all they knew, Mrs. Wilby might have supervised the packing of it. That was what Pauline called organization.

" Paul, you're a dear!" Val had just taken her basket when the other two came up: Corinna equipped with the famous wallet and the stout ash plant; and Julie encumbered with several most unbusinesslike parcels, through one of which cream oozed, while a horny claw protruded from another.

" It's a crab!" she cried triumphantly. " I'm standing a crab, and there's a perfect lettuce in one of these paper bags, and a few tomatoes, and salad dressing, and we'll have the most toothsome crab salad, as good as those you get in the French restaurants in Soho."

" Right," said Pauline. " And we'll have ten-minute shifts at getting the beast out of his shell. Then nobody's day will be ruined."

" I'll do it all," said Julie. " The crab salad's completely my show until it comes to eating it. It's not as good as lobster, of course, but——"

" Oh, it's quite good enough," said Pauline hastily, wanting to avoid the subject of Aileen. And as they entered the gate of the wood, more thickly overgrown and tangled now than in spring, but just as lovely, with trails of honeysuckle glimmering among the trees, and went along the turfy path, edged with tiny yellow and blue and purple flowers that clung close to the earth as if they were embroidered on it, Val almost forgot her anger with Aileen, almost wished Paul had agreed to let her come with them. It was all wrong that anyone should miss to-day—perhaps the place would never be so lovely again, and they would never be able to enjoy it in quite the same way.

" Val—Val—my dearest girl——"

Val's hat was suddenly jerked to the back of her head, and she almost dropped her basket, as a small figure sprang at her, clutched her tightly round the neck, and covered her face with hard and rather sticky kisses.

" Sammy!" she gasped. " Don't kill me."

" Well, I won't," said her former pupil, relaxing his embrace all at once. " But you deserve it, for going away from me like that. I've got a governess now, to teach me Latin, a proper one, and she pinched me once when I didn't understand the dative case, and I hate her!"

" I didn't want to go, Sammy," said Val, astonished at this outburst from the little boy, who had had time to forget her.

" Then why *did* you? Come back. Come back now, and then Mother'll send old Sturton away. And you won't know Spang, he's grown into a proper dog now, almost, and he killed a rat the other day, almost as big as an Angora rabbit—woo-oo-oof, you should have seen it. Come along *now*, come." And he pulled her so hard by the hand that she felt that her arm would be jerked from its socket.

" I can't come now. I'm going for a picnic with these girls, my friends. And what are you doing here all alone?"

" Ran away," said Sammy, nonchalantly, as if such a procedure were all in the day's work. " I always hate Saturday Latin, and I don't know that I shall go back."

From his demeanour Val guessed that he had not been long from home.

"I've got matches and a knife, and I'm going to cut down wood and make a fire."

"If you do that, my lad, the keeper'll put you in prison," said Julie.

"He won't. He knows me. He's my relation's keeper," said Sammy, drawing out his knife. "Look, Val, it's got a corkscrew."

"Shall we take him with us?" suggested Corinna, interested in Sammy's outfit.

"S-s-sh!" Pauline repressed her. "Look here, Sammy, you'd better cut off home. If you promise to go I'll give you these greengages."

"Are they ripe?" inquired Sammy doubtfully.

"I'll see him to the Tinkers' Dell turning," said Val. "You are going to the lake, aren't you? Come along, Sam. They're glorious greengages, all gold inside, and juicy, and we might give you a piece of chocolate too."

"We might," agreed Julie, dropping her parcels, and selecting the one likeliest to contain the required sweetmeat. "We'll give you anything but a crab's claw. That I refuse to part with."

The girls liberally contributed to the bribe, and at last Sammy was induced to turn towards home with Val. "If you stay we shan't forgive you," Pauline warned her. "The crab salad will be just about ready for you when you come back," promised Julie. " And the fire'll be going beautifully," said Corinna. It would have been quite good fun to help with the preparations for the picnic meal, especially with the fire, a delight even in the July heat, but, when once she and Sammy set off for Thornytangle, Val was reconciled to the rearrangement of the morning's plans. She was really glad to see the little boy again, to be able to send her love to the Mrs. Seyton who remembered so many things about Rose Faukner, and all of them good to hear, to be in touch again with people who had been friendly when she still felt friendless, and from whom she had been abruptly and unhappily separated. Sammy turned out his pockets for her entertainment, showing her both his new treasures and those she recognized as belonging to the past. Last of all came a small red pill-box, which he handed to her.

" You can have that, if you like," he said.

" Why? Is it full of pills?" asked Val, shaking it.

Sammy looked injured.

" Open it and see."

Expecting the worst, though what form it might take she did not know, Val very carefully removed the lid. Inside was a four-leaved clover.

" Sammy! the very thing I came to the wood to look for!" she exclaimed.

" Did you? Then now you've got it you can come home with me."

Val was about to concoct a tactful answer to this, when a figure in a pink print dress appeared at the edge of the wood. Sammy stopped short, furious-faced, and brandished his new knife.

" One step farther and I stab!" he shouted.

" Why, it's Ashdown!" Val and the little maid were so glad to see one another that Sammy's blood-thirsty threat was unnoticed, and, scowling, he snapped up the knife and pocketed it.

" I've thought about you so often and wondered if you was 'appy, Miss Val," declared Ashdown, hold-ing Val's hand in a rather moist grip. " I've struck oil in this place, and that's a fact. Of course Master Sammy is a bit of a nuisance sometimes, but 'e ain't so bad as a puppy, 'e's easier to catch, and 'e's got enough sense to keep 'isself from getting run over. The mistress is just a bit of all right. ' Gladys,' she says to me, ' Gladys, we'll put you in pink, acause pink suits you.' Fancy Mrs. Wilby saying that! If you looked well in a shade, it ud be the very reason for raising objections to it."

" I'll tell Mums you called her ' a bit of all right '," put in Sammy, desirous of getting at his present enemy in some way.

" She'd love to hear it," said Val. " Glad you're enjoying life, Ashdown."

" Ah, but, Miss Val, the p'int is, are you? At The Turret, I mean?"

" Oh, on and off." Val was rather embarrassed by the question, and the more so because it was followed by vigorous contortions on the part of Ashdown, who screwed up her face, worked her eyebrows, nodded, pursed up her mouth with a glance at Sammy, and otherwise indicated that she could a tale unfold, but not in his company.

" If you want to say something I'm not to hear, you needn't think I'm going away," said Sammy. " Because I'm not." And he wedged himself between Val and Ashdown, holding an arm of each.

" You're a naughty boy," said Ashdown, in the cheerful tone of one who makes the statement several times a day. " Well, Miss Val, I got my suspicions about something that ain't much to the credit of a certain person, and I shouldn't be surprised if we soon know oo's oo and w'at's w'at in a way that'll make the party in question sit up. See you later. Ta-ta."

With a practised hand she seized Sammy before he had time to dart away again into the depths of the wood. He clawed and fought, used strong expressions about the unfortunate Miss Sturton, declared that he knew what his mother wanted, and no one else did, implored Val to take him back to the picnic, and finally, feeling himself towed in a homeward direction by the gradually prevailing strength of the small but wiry Ashdown, flung himself on the ground and burst into loud yells of fury.

" You just go back, Miss Val," advised Ashdown. " 'E's conquered. 'Ome my lord goes, though I 'ave to drag 'im all the way, and 'is trousers'll be ruined. Get up, now, Master Sammy, and try to be'ave like a little gentleman."

The very notion of such a thing incited Sammy to a fresh outburst, and Val, though with a guilty sense of abandoning Ashdown in time of trouble, accepted her advice, and hurried back to the lake.

A delicious meal was spread on a turfy mound sprinkled with daisies, and near it the bright tongue of a little fire darted and flickered between two stones. Corinna had boiled the billy can and made some sort of beverage, which she declared to be entirely essential to the outdoor life, and to combine the good qualities of tea, bovril, coffee, cocoa, milk, and ginger beer. It was of a strange colour, and seemed extremely hot, but she drank it with resolution. The others preferred lemonade, made of pink and yellow powder and water from the spring. The salad was declared a great success, though Julie had found much difficulty in extracting meat from claws and shell, and, whenever there was a pause in the conversation, exclaimed in mournful tones—" I was *swindled* over that crab." Pauline had put by a reserve stock of food for tea, and refused to allow access to the basket which contained it, providentially hidden among the fern, in a place known only to herself. When the girls had eaten every available scrap of lunch they lay and talked, the easy lazy talk of out-of-doors, with other talk coming into it without disturbance: the whisper of the light wind in the leaves, the slow ripple of the water in the reeds, the drone of the heavy bees, the little stirrings and rustlings in the wood which make it so easy to believe in fairies and dryads, stealing unseen about their tasks among the trees. After a dreamy hour, they suddenly became vigorous, and raced and skimmed stones and bathed; and then they found that it was time for tea, and Corinna rekindled the fire, and Pauline brought out the hidden hoard, and again they feasted, their delight in the lovely place and the lazy day growing greater and keener. " To camp here for the summer," said Val, " would be the best thing that could happen to anyone."

All but Val had been told to be home by eight, and all forgot the passing of time. It was Pauline who first remembered, and, jerking up her hand to see her wrist watch, announced in an incredulous voice that it was five and twenty to nine.

" Your watch must be wrong," said Corinna, who hadn't one.

" My watch is never wrong," said Pauline.

" It *is* that hour." Julie held her watch to her ear.

" What an oversight!   There'll be alarums and excursions at home.'

" We'll walk to Lyncote station," arranged Pauline
quickly. " That won't take much over twenty minutes,
if we hurry. There's a short cut to the station lane.
I believe there's a train somewhere about nine—with
luck we might manage to catch it."

" I'll come a little way with you, but I'll walk home,"
said Val, who was as penniless as she had been before
the Thornytangle episode.

" If you must, start now," said Pauline, abruptly,
because she hated the thought of Val going off by
herself and yet could not offer to accompany her, as
" being home in time " was one of the rules on which
her people laid stress. " There'll be no fun in sprinting
with us to the station: it'll be mere waste of time.
Good-bye."

They hurried off, and Val, left to herself, experienced
the sensation familiar to everyone who has walked
through the woods in the late evening alone. Where
sparkling light had danced over friendly shade was
now deep in sinister shadow, the tree-trunks, cold and
colourless as grey stone, seemed to stand in wait,
eyeless and yet watchful; happy sounds of the sunny
day had gone, and the occasional furtive stir of some
little night hunter in the old fallen leaves of last year
made Val start as if she were the object of his search,
instead of the dreaded human from whom he would

have scuttled away in terror. Strange shapes appeared where there had been only stumps or wind-blown trees: a hunched clumsy figure—of what? a long thin dancer with arms flung out and one foot poised for the shuffle that never came, a fugitive ready to dash from the fetters of his captors, and unable to move. " It's just as if all the feelings people have in woods were turned into shapes and left here," thought Val, trying to entertain herself, and resolutely forcing herself to walk slowly, sure that if she were to quicken her pace she would run, and if she ran—she did not know, but she knew instinctively that she must not do it.

Suddenly a light wind went through the trees, and the wood changed its shape. " Now it's going to run after me," said Val to herself. " No, it *isn't*. It's going to run away from me." And then, borne on the wind, came the friendly delicious fragrance of burning wood. " A camp-fire," thought Val, welcoming it at first, doubtful of its desirability as she remembered that it might come from a gipsy encampment — she had never much cared for gipsies — or warm some criminal escaped from justice, afraid to kindle a fire by day. It was a very strong smell, though—it must be a good big fire—no one who didn't want to call attention to himself would light such a huge one.

" Val!"

" *Oh!* " It was quite a small squeak, but it was out before Val had time to suppress it.

" Aileen!" She recovered herself. " What on earth are you wandering about here alone for?"

" Val!" Aileen caught hold of her arm. " There's a fire over there—an awful fire—it'll spread over the whole wood—it'll burn Rookmere—it'll burn our house, perhaps. The wind's blowing it in that direction. It's a terribly long way to the keeper's cottage—it's simply rushing on with this wind—what shall we do?"

Even in the excitement of the moment, Val noticed that " what shall *we* do?" It made her feel friendlier towards Aileen than she had done for some time, a lot friendlier.

" Show me—quick—where is it?"

They hurried down a side path through a small plantation of young larch trees to a space of bracken and heather, tinder after a fortnight of dry weather. Evidently a fire had been lighted on the far side of this, under two magnificent oaks, whose meeting branches made a canopy over a little hillock, a favourite place for privileged picnickers, and near enough to a road to tempt trespassers, willing, for the beauty of the place, to risk an interview with a keeper and threats of prosecution. Left smouldering, the fire must have blazed into life with the wind, which drove it towards the heather. Val gasped as she saw it leaping on, its flames now like a hundred long tongues, now leaping up like slim pennons of red and gold, now joined in what seemed a solid mass of live shining fire.

" Water—where can we get water?" cried Aileen.

" Is water much good for a fire like that? We could never carry enough. Don't men beat it out?" Val glanced round distractedly. " The larches! Aileen, it mustn't get to that larch wood! Don't you know how larch twigs burn in a picnic fire? It'll destroy every tree in it—it'll burn on and on, and nothing, nothing will be able to stop it."

" I know—that's what I told you—that's what it'll be." Aileen's voice was high and trembling, but she had control of herself. Like Val, she wanted to do the right thing, the efficient thing. If they could only think of it, they would get ahead with it, at once, whatever it was, however dangerous and hard.

" We can't stop it where it is—we must stop it from going more than a certain distance. I remember! I know! You dig a trench, Aileen, that stops it—just here, before it gets to the larch wood. No good where the heather is, that's too hard. This is a squashy bit —come on. Why, look! It's a ditch. But it's full of dry stuff—if we clear all that out——"

Val began to dig away with her hands, like a new sort of mole or beaver, working furiously, with very little result.

' I know! Some young men are coming down here

to camp—they were making preparations the other day—they may have left spades——"

"Tear along and see! They can't be there—they'd have smelt the fire by now—but go and see if they've left anything," panted Val, giving up her attempts to scoop out the ditch, and wrenching up heather and bracken in the path of the fire.

Aileen darted off. In five minutes, which seemed to the desperately labouring Val like an hour, she was back, carrying a spade.

"They've left it!" she gasped. "They're not there, but this, and a few more camping things——"

"Now we'll do it!" Val seized the spade and drove it into the ditch. "You tear up the heather, Aileen, as well as you can, I'll carry on with this for a bit."

Faces blackened, hands bleeding and bruised, bodies trembling with the strain of carrying out endeavour on which so much depended, the two girls worked like navvies. Val was tough, and Aileen, though she sometimes affected delicacy, had strength, and sense enough to use it wisely. As they laboured together, they were getting to know one another in a way that they would never forget, though, at the time, they were hardly conscious of one another's presence. They did not seem like individuals, but one force resisting the dreadful force of the fire. When Aileen again rushed away, Val did not look up or question her as to where she was going. It was as if she felt instinctively that she was doing something to serve this joint effort of theirs. And she was right. Aileen came staggering back with two canvas buckets, three-quarters full of water.

"I've spilt some — one at a time — might be better."

"What luck!—Quick, Aileen! On the fire!"

"In the trench first."

In sloshed the water, and Val flung down the spade.

"Take a turn at this. I'll fetch the next lot."

"Spring's a few steps to left of bell tent."

"Right."

In the depths of the wood it grew dark, but the camp way could be distinguished in the dusk of the late summer evening. The ditch cleared, the girls toiled together for water. At last, drenched and aching from head to foot, they knew they were conquering the fire. Here and there an enterprising little flame coiled forward, only to be at once stamped out, or to sizzle into nothingness. The advance of the fire checked, theirs began. Patch after patch of flame was beaten out, extinguished. The trees no longer stood out clearly, illumined by the splendid glare of flame, but shrank back into an indefinite crowded mass, dark in the faint light of the moon. In the black, devastated stretch between oaks and larches not a point or ribbon of fire was to be seen. Val straightened herself with a groan, pressing her hands to her aching back.

" The end of a perfect day," she said. " I wonder what Mrs. Wilby will think. It must be midnight."

" You must stay the night with us. We'll phone down to The Turret."

Val considered quickly. It seemed the only thing to be done.

" Won't your people be scared?" she said. " Won't they wonder what has become of you?"

" They're dining out, or were. They'll probably think I'm in bed and asleep."

" They'll get a rude awakening, won't they? Do you often wander about in the Rookmere woods alone?"

" Just when the mood takes me—I thought I might meet you—I rather wanted to see you, you know. Val—you've been so different lately."

" Well, if I have, you made me," returned Val. " However, we'll discuss that later. I say—I do not like coming to your place at this time and in this state. What will your mother think?"

" Oh, Mother always understands when I want her to," said Aileen. " Aunt Carol's the crux. But she'll probably be in bed—anyway, we'll hope so."

The girls did not say much more as they hurried through the wood. Val's mind was in a tangle with the confusion of the day's events: the meeting with Sammy; Ashdown's mysterious hints; the lovely calm coloured hours by the lake, that seemed so long ago; the unexpected encounter with Aileen, and the fight with the fire. All these things were of importance to her, and she wondered dully why she couldn't give much attention to any of them, but was chiefly conscious of being dog-tired. Striding along by Aileen, she thrust one hand into her blazer pocket. Her fingers closed over a small round object—Sammy's pill-box, and, within it, safely shut away, her talisman of luck, Sammy's four-leaved clover.

CHAPTER XVII

Unexpected Developments

Mrs. Ellerton received the girls without any reproaches. Her welcome might have been different had she known beforehand that Aileen was stamping out a fire in the Rookmere woods instead of being safely asleep, but, not having suffered from racked nerves, she was disposed to regard the whole affair as a daring and heroic adventure, and to feel that her child deserved some sort of medal from some shadowy society for her pluck and endurance. Val, guiltily aware that, whatever the circumstances, she would have been scolded at home for so late a return, stood by listening while anxious and loving questions were put, and rather curt and impatient answers given, until Miss Ellerton, who no one had thought knew anything of the matter, strode in with the information that she had telephoned to Mrs. Wilby and set her mind at ease about Val.

" Better have a bath and get off to bed," she snapped, cutting short Mrs. Ellerton's breathless account of what they had been through. And in less than half an hour Val, comforted by a warm spray and plunge in a bath deliciously scented with rose-coloured crystals, found herself lying between cool linen sheets in a little guest-room, which, tired as she was, she realized to be the perfection of its kind. " I don't know whether it's the best luck in the world to *be* a pet," she thought, " but it's quite good to be friendly with one, some-times." And with this worldly reflection she fell asleep.

Aileen walked part of the way home with her next morning. They inspected the blackened patch which bore witness to last night's fire, and were astonished to find that the devastation was not so great, or the ditch they had cleared so deep and wide, as they had thought in the fear and confusion of their adventure. " All the same, Mr. Hayling will be furious," said Aileen. " He thinks that all picnickers do damage. Towards the end of every season he refuses to give people per-mission even to walk through Rookmere."

" I wonder who set that fire going," said Val. " We didn't see any picnic party except our own."

" It couldn't have been your fire, could it?" said Aileen.

" Why, no. We camped by the lake all day, and Pauline and Corinna poured kettles of water on ours," said Val. " There couldn't be any question about our being responsible."

" I'm glad of that," said Aileen. " I won't come

any farther with you, Val. It's too hot. Good-bye—
I'll see you at school on Monday."

Val nodded gaily, but went on her way feeling in
rather low spirits. Always Mrs. Wilby seemed to
find her unpleasant and tiresome, and, now there was
real cause for annoyance, she prepared for the worst.
" I must just accept it without making a fuss," she
warned herself. " Mother would be angry with me."
She remembered, when she was little, having been
sent to bed at three in the afternoon for having cut
luncheon and stayed out to play with a family of
children who, like Aileen, might come in to meals
or not, as they chose. " Bed in broad daylight's the
worst," she thought. " And, whatever the worst
is, it'll be over by this time to-morrow."

It wasn't. But, among all her speculations, Val had
not guessed what it would be. Mrs. Wilby met her
with a woeful face—in fact, for one dreadful moment,
Val's thoughts flew to the fear that was never far
distant—the fear lest her mother's health should have
grown worse again. That, at any rate, was short-
lived.

" How did it happen that you were so careless?"
exclaimed Mrs. Wilby, in low tones, as if resolved that
the inmates of the houses flanking The Turret should
hear nothing. " I've done my best—I caught the early
morning train and apologized for you to Mr. Hayling,
but he was very much put out, I could see that. I

only hope the matter will go no further. I'm afraid Miss Beauchamp and the school authorities will hear of it, as yours was, in effect, a school picnic."

" Put out! But he ought to be jolly grateful!" cried Val, too completely astounded to remember the neighbours, whose ears, one would imagine from Mrs. Wilby's repeated warnings, were constantly stretched to hear any detail of any conversation, however uninteresting, that took place in The Turret. " Why, I should have been back here in fairly good time if I hadn't stayed in the wood to put out that fire. Aileen and I—why, her mother seems to think that she should have a gold medal."

" Aileen was not picnicking with you, I understood from Miss Ellerton's message. Was she?"

" No, she wasn't, but——"

" In that case the child does perhaps deserve a little praise for helping to put out a fire caused by your carelessness."

" But it wasn't our fire!" cried Val in desperation. " It was in quite a different place—it was by the oaks, and ours was by the lake. Ask Pauline, or Julie, or Corinna Shaw—they know where we lit it."

The placidity of Mrs. Wilby's cameo profile was slightly marred by a look Val was beginning to know well—a look of faintly disgusted incredulity.

" I understand your companions came home by train, and you walked through the woods alone."

"Of course I did! I hadn't the train fare!" cried Val, forgetting all her resolutions to be patient, half distracted with the fears and suggestions that began to crowd upon her. "But why should I light a fire at that time, all by myself? Why, I hadn't even a box of matches."

Mrs. Wilby looked down at her hands.

"I must say I can hardly credit your mother's daughter with being guilty of an act of wanton destruction," she said in a low even voice. "I quite believe that the whole affair was an accident—however it happened. And you certainly had the decency to extinguish the fire—not before a very beautiful place had been spoiled and made unsightly. I have done what I can for you. My apology may avert a formal complaint to Miss Beauchamp. It might be more efficacious if followed by a written apology from you."

"I can't apologize!" said Val. "I'm not going to tell Mr. Seton Hayling that I'm sorry for starting a fire when he should tell me he's glad I helped to put it out."

Mrs. Wilby took Val's wrist between gentle, warm fingers.

"Val, dear! Are you sure? Think over your day at Rookmere. Could you swear in a court of law that no fire you lighted, no spark blown from that fire, could have done the damage of which Miss Ellerton told me?"

The light touch of the fingers became a grip. Val jerked her hand away. Her breath caught a little, as if she were frightened.

" I'm as sure as one can be of anything," she said, rather unsteadily. " And there isn't any damage done —not any to speak of. No timber went. The place will be as pretty as ever next year."

" Now, that's the spirit I can't bear to see in you," said Mrs. Wilby quite sharply. " For your own sake you should try to change it. It will do you no good, and might do you a great deal of harm."

Val said no more. Resentful and a little scared, she dragged dully through the routine of the day. It seemed interminable. She wanted to go round and see Pauline, and warn her of Miss Beauchamp's possible questions about the fire, but her guardian wished her to stay in, and she did not try to persuade her to change her mind. She was beginning to feel that anything of the kind would be as hopeless as to reason with a great feather pillow or wad of cotton wool which was choking her. At last the day passed, and the night tacked to it, and Monday came with its welcome school, and Pauline, and Julie, and Corinna. But directly Val entered the building she was told to go to Miss Beauchamp's room. She looked round in vain for one of her fellow-picnickers, and guessed rightly that they had already been sent for. When, with all the restrained agitation usual in such circumstances, she entered the presence of the head mistress, she found them ranged before her desk.

" Now, Valentine, what's all this about a fire?" said Miss Beauchamp, in her curt but not unpleasant voice. " You put a fire out, I understand?"

" Yes—Aileen Ellerton and I did."

" And Mr. Hayling appears to think that you were also responsible for lighting it. I have a letter from him "—Miss Beauchamp took it up from her desk— " in which he says that the damage is not great, but that it might have been considerable—and he very naturally considers that the privilege of a permit carries certain responsibilities, which should be recognized. You all agree to that, I suppose."

" Yes," said the four at once.

" It really wasn't our fire," said Pauline.

" I don't know why Mr. Hayling should write like his."

" It was my guardian's mistake, I think," said Val. ' She got hold of the wrong story, and apologized for ny having set the wood on fire before she knew that I'd only helped to put a small piece of it out."

" Tell me exactly what did happen," said Miss Beauchamp.

Val stated her case. The head mistress made few comments. Not one of the four knew what her opinion was, whether she was inclined to believe the tale or

not. But, thought Val, her mind did not close down
on yours—you could say what you had done, and
leave it at that, to be judged for what it was worth.
There was no twisting or distorting or leaping to
conclusions, no sudden panic driving you to what
seemed like insolence or sulkiness. When they were
dismissed, she went with a sense of relief, as if things
must ultimately work out at their own value. She gave
Aileen, waiting outside, a little nod of reassurance.
The others did not share her sentiments. They were
in a state of full-blown agitation, and much was said
and threatened before Pauline drew Val away by herself.

" I've got a pretty strong suspicion as to who started
that fire," she said.

For one minute Val thought the accusing finger was
to be pointed at her, and stared at Pauline with troubled
eyes. But she was mistaken.

" Who, Paul?"

" Aileen Ellerton herself."

" Oh, no. Why should she?"

" I don't think she'd do it out of sheer malice, to
involve us in the blame," said Pauline. " Though
when people go about saying ' I hate you ' one can
believe almost anything of them. I think she was
prowling round all day, or all the afternoon, in the
hope of seeing you and having a grand reconciliation.
She probably made herself picnic tea, and forgot the

fire, and was in a fair funk about it when she saw it spreading."

Val was silent, thinking.

" Well?" said Pauline, with the slight impatience of those who are not quite certain of theories which it would be convenient to prove true. " Doesn't it seem pretty sound?"

" Y-y-yes, but I don't think it *is*. I think Aileen's all right underneath, you know."

" So's everybody, if you get far enough down. Only it means getting to the bones sometimes," said Pauline.

Val smiled, rather wryly, thinking of Mrs. Wilby. She wondered if that lady would want to know what had been said at school about the Rookmere fire, and decided that she would not. She never really wanted to know about anything: her mind was always made up, and her questions asked merely to prove an unalterable conclusion. But this time Mrs. Wilby did make inquiries. Was Val in trouble at school? Had Miss Beauchamp said anything?

" If I'm in trouble Aileen is in with me," said Val. " The girls know I hadn't matches."

Mrs. Wilby primmed up her mouth, and hoped Val wasn't trying to shift the responsibility on to other shoulders. It would be all right, declared Val, Miss Beauchamp would hit on some satisfactory solution, and in the end Mr. Hayling would bear no ill-will towards the Myra Dakin girls. " That's all we hope for now," she added, whimsically, but rather miserably. "We actually thought he'd be pleased with us once."

Miss Beauchamp said no more about the episode, evidently regarding the case as not proven. But on Wednesday Pauline came to school in high indignation. She had had a note from the bailiff of the estate, asking her to return the permit—evidently in case she should use it on some other date.

"Just as we had planned that gorgeous camping holiday!" she said. "We should have had it, you know—one permit leads to another."

"Don't you think we shall ever be allowed to go there again?" said Corinna, looking very melancholy. "I was sure of that summer holiday. I overhauled my kit last night, and Father gave me one of his old fishing-rods. Think of grilling trout on the stones."

The others let Corinna think of it. They were so much depressed by the realization of the loss of the place with which they had fallen so deeply in love that it did not seem worth while to point out that the reality, with luck, might be the boiling of small roach or bits of bream in the billy.

"I don't think Mr. Seton Hayling would have let you camp anyway," said Aileen, evidently trying to cheer up the disconsolate ones.

"Don't you? Why?"

" He doesn't often allow people to picnic there."

Pauline groaned, thinking of her permit, on its imposing light blue paper.

" Are *you* allowed to wander about there doing any damage you like?" she said abruptly. " Or have you special permission?"

Aileen flushed.

" Many people consider that grassy drive a right of way," she said.

" They do. That's probably the trouble."

" Do you remember, Corinna? You and I went that way to Lyncote," said Val, hardly knowing why she was anxious to change the subject.

" Look here, Aileen,"—Pauline refused to follow the turn of the conversation. " You found that fire. You told Val about it. There was nobody else, as far as we know, in Rookmere woods all day."

" As far as you know," said Aileen huffily. " That's not very far."

" Farther than you think, perhaps. But we should like to know, very much, if you lighted a fire in Rook-mere on Saturday."

" I daresay you would," said Aileen, a little nerve twitching in one cheek. " I suppose you suspect me of setting the place on fire."

There was a silence. Julie and Corinna looked curiously at Aileen; Pauline stared at a brown trail of faded laburnum flowers outside the window; Val regarded the shiny lid of her desk. She wished Pauline would let the thing drop.

" It's a pity Aileen and I found that old fire!" she exclaimed. " When I think of how we slaved to put it out——"

" *You* didn't find it," said Pauline, " You were told about it."

" I'm dead sick of it, anyhow. Let's leave it alone, and forget Rookmere. You're a Stoic, Paul, you can easily do that."

" There are some things beyond Stoics," snapped Pauline. " I don't believe there's a place in this country like Rookmere—it's the uttermost edge to lose it as we've done, without saying a word, through no fault of our own."

" I wonder if it would do any good if *I* went up to Mr. Hayling and explained," said Val doubtfully, realizing that the explanation which might have been quite simple became complicated when it involved contradiction of Mrs. Wilby's polite apology.

" You aren't the one to go. Aileen found the fire, and knows all about it. She's the person to explain."

They looked at Aileen. Her people probably knew Mr. Hayling—it wouldn't be difficult for her to call and tell him how it happened, and it might have good results. For a minute Val thought she was going to say carelessly—" Of course I'll go," and put herself right with the Fifth. She did not realize that, like many girls much petted at home, Aileen suffered from overwhelming shyness, and would sooner have thought of adventuring into the castle of an ogre to explain why she should not be eaten than of visiting Mr. Hayling to put before him what she knew of the facts of an episode which had annoyed him.   She drew herself up with the haughty gesture which alternately amused and irritated the Fifth.

"That's your point of view," she said.   "But I shall explain nothing."

CHAPTER XVIII

Banishment and Welcome

A real friendship was growing up between Pauline and Val, and it was not possible that they should be estranged as easily as schoolgirls who think they like one another very much sometimes are, but Pauline was a little irritated with Val for not following up her theories about Aileen's part in the fire, or, at any rate, not urging her to explain to Mr. Hayling what actually had happened, and so to clear the picnickers from suspicion, and perhaps build again the hope of that summer camp, even more precious now it seemed shattered. Val felt at once that there was something wrong—nothing much, but enough constantly to irritate with reminders of its existence, as a hurt finger or a cut lip will do. It would come right again, she felt sure of that, but she did not like it. Most gratefully she accepted Aileen's suggestion that she should come up to Lyncote on Saturday, play tennis, or lounge by the stream if the sun's glare was fierce on the courts, and have tea. Mrs. and Miss Ellerton were always kind to Val, the one because Aileen liked her, the other because she herself did, and, after all the bursts of petulance and the misunderstandings of the past weeks, it seemed as if the sense of kinship which the two new girls had felt early in the term, on that afternoon in the orchard, was again reasserting itself. " I don't believe Aileen will say ' I hate you ' again," thought Val, as, after an early and very meagre luncheon, she trudged the white dusty road to Lyncote. " And I don't believe a word about her tale-tellings to get the part of Viola. Pauline's far too clever about that. Of course Paul doesn't know Mrs. Wilby, not properly. She probably wouldn't believe in her if I tried to explain her—I don't think anyone would. I don't myself when I'm not at The Turret—I just forget."

But that afternoon Val remembered. As she neared the hospitably open gate of Lyncote, she was met by Mrs. Ellerton.

" I thought it was you coming along the road," she said, rushing on her words, though she spoke in her usual languid voice. " I ran down to meet you, because I was resolved to see you before Nina should meet you or suspect anything, resolved upon it."

She paused, panting a little. Her garden hat had slipped far back on her head, she had forgotten to remove a dab of powder from one cheek, her eyes glittered with nervous excitement. Val felt rather frightened, and sorry for her.

" Is Aileen ill?" she asked at once.

" No, she's not ill, but, poor childie, I can't understand why she is not, after all she has gone through
during the last few days. Those wicked girls! They
ought to be severely punished, accusing her in such
a way, when she acted like a little heroine! And you,
Val, you've always pretended to be her friend—how
could you set such a cruel, cruel story afoot about
her?"

" I don't understand," stammered poor Val, crimson.

"That is what false friends always say. Poor child:
I don't believe she would credit one word against you.
But I made up my mind that you should know that I
know the whole story. I don't believe in letting anyone,
however young, behave falsely and cruelly and spite-
fully without saying one word of condemnation."

" But, Mrs. Ellerton, you're all wrong! I haven't
said one word against Aileen! If it's that fuss about
the fire you're speaking of, it's really all right. The
girls are just irritated because they've lost the chance
of camping at Rookmere—they'll forget about it. It'll
be all right, really."

Mrs. Ellerton hardly seemed to hear her. Evidently
it was by so great an effort that she had strung herself
up to say what was in her mind that she was unable to
stop until she had said it all.

" It's wrong, you know, Val, to let jealousy get
such a hold of you that you'll invent such cruel stories

about people. It wasn't Nina's fault that she took the part of Viola from you—Mrs. Wilby suspected that you were neglecting your work, and was terribly upset to hear that Miss Dymchurch was obliged to speak to you so sharply before the class. I was quite sorry to have said anything about it, when I saw how much it distressed her, and——"

" Did Mrs. Wilby call on you yesterday?" broke in Val, struck with a new idea, and so miserably eager to find out if it were true that she forgot to apologize for her interruption.

But Mrs. Ellerton went on with her reproaches.

" I'm sorry not to see Aileen," said Val, trying to steady her voice. " What you think is wrong—if Mrs. Wilby told you she's quite mistaken. She does make mistakes. You'll find out some time." And she turned and fled ignominiously, afraid lest she should break down, for the shock of this reception, compared with the gentle lavish hospitality she had expected, was the kind that makes people many years older than Val feel inclined to cry.

" What is going to happen to me?" she thought. " It doesn't seem real—it seems like a fairy tale, where everything that looks delightful turns out all wrong. Perhaps fairy tales are really the true ones. What heat this is! Why didn't I go to that spring where Corinna camped that day and have a drink?" She felt in her blazer pocket to discover if a threepenny bit might lurk in a corner. There was no threepenny bit: she knew there wouldn't be, but her fingers found a trophy she had quite forgotten—the pill-box with the four-leaved clover.

" Luck!" she thought. " Sammy must have found this under an unlucky star. Things have really got rather worse since he gave it to me."

Then, all of a sudden, she remembered Ashdown's vague hints. " I got my suspicions about something that ain't much to the credit of a certain person—I shouldn't be surprised if we soon know oo's oo and w'at's w'at in a way that'll make the party in question sit up." What did she mean? That the " party in question " was Mrs. Wilby there couldn't be much doubt. Was there anything in it? " It isn't done and it won't do." She could hear her mother snapping it out as comment on certain things. And one of these things was gossiping with someone else's maid, however much you might like her. Anyway, Ashdown wasn't Mrs. Wilby's maid now. And Val, in the new loneliness that came with this estrangement from Aileen's people, felt desperate, ready to snatch at any hope.

Could she call at Thornytangle? Could she tell Mrs. Seyton how badly things were going with her? Her mother had advised her not to lift up her voice in complaint to outsiders directly she felt at variance with her present guardian. But it wasn't that something little was wrong, it was something big, something that wouldn't put itself right easily. Escape was the only hope. To get away—to know that she would never enter The Turret again—it seemed freedom beyond dreams.

Without realizing it, she took the familiar turning to Tinkers' Dell, and walked towards Thornytangle. She had not gone far down the deep lane, always dampish and cool between its high leafy banks, before she saw a well-known figure in a pink print dress and a black straw hat, standing in an attitude of expostulation and despair.

" If you don't come down this minute, Master Sammy, I'll turn the wasps' nest on to you."

Val looked up, and saw another figure, equally familiar, clinging to one of the branches that overarched the lane. Something in the way he held on suggested panic rather than disobedience, and Val guessed that persuasion might be more effective than threats.

" What's wrong with him?" she asked, approaching Ashdown.

" Ow, Miss Val, the very person I was wanting to see. 'E's a downright nuisance, isn't 'e? I never saw such a naughty boy. First of all it was the wasps' nest, and a nice job I had getting him past it. As it was 'e threw a stone, and one or two popped out, but we run like the wind, and they didn't notice us.

And now my lord's up there, and come down 'e will not, and tea at five and all."

"I don't believe he *can* come down," said Val softly. And, raising her voice—"Sammy—hullo, Sammy!"

"Hullo!" responded Sammy, rather distantly, as if he were thinking of something else.

"Come down and let's have a look at you."

No answer.

"Will you come if I come up and fetch you?"

Still no answer, but Sammy's expression, as far as Val could make out, indicated that he was not altogether hostile to the idea. She climbed the bank, mounted the enormous tangle of the torn-up root that had attracted Sammy, swung herself from it, as he had done, into the low arching bough of another tree, and crept along to where he sat. It was nothing of a climb, but, looking down into the deep passage of the lane, Val could understand his sudden paralysing fright. Unexpectedly, all of a sudden, one seemed so far above the safe surface of the earth, and forgot how near the tree root at the top of the bank was, and how quickly it was possible to creep back to it again.

"Come along, Sam! Come and sit by me *here*," she invited, settling herself a short distance from him. "There isn't room for me where you are."

The near presence of someone else, and her matter-of-fact way of speaking, broke the spell of fright that had settled on the little boy. He crawled to where Val sat, and she moved along, nearer the bank and safety. Once he had stirred from his place on the bough it was not difficult to persuade him to climb along and down. Though he had regained confidence in himself, the memory of his sudden panic was strong enough to make him quite willing to be on earth. Ashdown gave him a small shake of greeting.

" W'en you're a mangled 'eap you'll be sorry," she informed him. " But never mind 'im, Miss Val. Just you go and wash your faceanands in that trough, Master Sam. What I want to say is this—it ain't fair that Mrs. Wilby should be 'alf starving you and not giving you a mite of pocket-money when she gets what she does for keeping you."

" But, Ashdown, she doesn't get much!" said Val in surprise. " We're jolly hard up, since the failure of Marraby's, you know."

" Well, Miss Val, that's where you make the mistake. She wasn't well w'en one cheque for you come, and she sent me out to cash it. It was a lot of money— twenty pounds, it was. And I didn't think of it in connection with you, till you 'appened to mention that funny name, Mr. John 'Unniker. And then I didn't think much about it——"

" But, Ashdown, twenty pounds doesn't go very far for all expenses, you know," said Val.

" Twenty pounds by itself is nothing nowadays,"

D 503

AN ATTITUDE OF EXPOSTULATION AND DESPAIR

Page 214

said Ashdown firmly. " But you listen a bit, Miss
Val. I just 'appened to be in Lloyd's 'anding in some
books for the missus—she just 'ates going in to Dakin
Priors, you know—and oo should I see but my lady,
sailin' in like the royal family to cash another cheque.
She doesn't see me, but I keeps my eagle eye fixed,
you bet. And when she drops a bit of blue paper that
was round the cheque I pounces, and 'ands it back, as
if to a perfect stranger, polite as you like, but not
afore I see what was written on it——"

Ashdown paused dramatically.

" What was it?"

" I can't remember the exact words, but it was
something like ' Paid to Mrs. Florence Wilby, for
board, lodging, and pocket-money for Valentine
Forrest—John Hunniker '. And it was another twenty
pounds. Not so long after the first."

Val gazed at Ashdown, astounded.

" Are you *sure*?"

Ashdown made some rapid signs, which seemed to
suggest that she was quite willing that anyone who
cared should cut her throat were she not speaking the
exact truth.

" You don't catch me repeating a thing I only know
'arf and 'arf, so to speak," she said. " I said to myself
—' I 'ave my suspicions and I'll 'ave further proof.
Artful my lady may be, but she's not the only artful
one,' said I. " I've fair 'aunted that bank, Miss Val.

There was the cheque I cashed meself; there was the cheque I seen her cash; there was the June one, cashed with yours truly watching in a corner——"

Ashdown's sharp little face was more than usually alive with excitement and triumph.

" So you see, Miss Val, you ought to 'ave plenty of pocket-money for your games and that, and live on the fat of the land," she said.

" I don't know about that," said Val, thinking. Like most girls, she had a rather vague idea as to living expenses, but it certainly seemed as if Mr. Hunniker were allowing a decent sum towards them. Up till now she had imagined it to be practically non-existent, had thought she was living on the charity of her mother's old friend, her guardian.

" I wonder if Mother knows," she said. " She's been ill, and I haven't been able to write to her much —and not at all about myself."

" You bet your boots she *don't*," said Ashdown. " But she oughter—and she will."

" Oh, don't write to her just now, Ashdown," cried Val. " If she thought I was unhappy it might worry her to death."

" So you are un'appy, are you?" said Ashdown. " Don't you worry about givin' it away, Miss Val. I knew it. I've known it ever since I was in The Turret with you, and I was bound to, knowing as I did 'ow that Mrs. Wilby could make you feel. I tell you, Miss

Val, I've been that 'ungry I could have chewed the door-mat or the boots. And ' That will do, Ashdown. You may go, Ashdown ', and 'er miserable bit of 'ash on a silver dish."

" I wonder if she's terribly poor," said Val.

" Poor! She ain't poor, Miss Val. She can afford to 'ave a real good blow-out at the café when she feels like it, and she feels like it fairly often, I can tell you. She's too poor to let other people 'ave things, even their own—that's 'er sort of poorness, and it's the sort that can be 'elped and ought to be stopped."

" But what can we do?" said Val.

" You say writing to your mother's out of the question, Miss Val. But there was nothing wrong with a postcard or two to Mr. John 'Unniker, I trust? From a Friend and Well-wisher. . . . Oh, you needn't be afraid, 'e won't think it's your writing, I just wish 'e would—I never could write, it's more like a spider than a yooman being."

Val felt a small hand clasp hers, and looked down to see Sammy. How much he had taken in she did not know, but he was looking extremely worried. She laughed, and gave him a little pat.

" Keep calm, Sam," she said. " Everything's all right in the end, isn't it?"

" I shan't keep calm if you don't come back to tea," said Sammy vigorously.

"I can't come to-day, Sam. Mrs. Seyton won't be expecting me. I'll come some time next week."

"But Mrs. Seyton *will* be expecting you—and has been for a very long time," said a deep cheerful voice, and, starting round, Val saw Mrs. Seyton herself, more sunburnt than ever, and her blue eyes even friendlier than they had been when she first spoke of Rose Faukner.

"Oh, I *am* glad to see you!" Val couldn't find anything else to say, and, of course, she couldn't have found anything better.

"And how are you? Looking a bit washed out— time for the holidays, evidently. And how's your mother? I'm really offended with you, Val, though I mayn't seem so. Your guardian promised that you should come up and see us. Even though you couldn't give us your professional services we hoped you'd come friendly-wise."

Val flushed indignantly, remembering how emphatically Mrs. Wilby had declared she was not to visit Thornytangle, as she would not be wanted there.

"I didn't get the message," she said curtly.

Mrs. Seyton looked at her quickly.

"Well—come along now. Or do you think you will be expected at home?"

"No. I said I was going to Lyncote—but it didn't come off."

Mrs. Seyton asked no more questions, and Sammy,

running before Val, dragged her along in triumph, while Ashdown, grinning broadly and sympathetically, followed in the rear. It was good to pass the tangled hedge again, to be welcomed riotously by Spang, now the size of a grown-up dog, and to enter the friendly hall, with its books, its deep settee, and the great stone jar, filled with poppies now, bright and huge, their petals stretched wide, but not fallen.

" Tell me what you're doing," said Mrs. Seyton, when, tea over, they sat in the garden, pretending to be engrossed in the exhibition of tricks which Sam declared Spangie really could perform, and which he had never been known to shirk until this moment. " How's school—are you top of the Fifth?"

" No—Pauline beats me. She's very clever, you know."

" She must be," laughed Mrs. Seyton. " And what about this *Twelfth Night*? You are Viola, aren't you?"

" I was. I pretend to be sometimes. I'm out, though. Aileen Ellerton's doing it."

" Oh! I had a letter from your mother the other day —she says you don't write as much as you did."

" I couldn't. I wasn't allowed to," said Val quickly.

" No. Of course not."

" Jump, Spang! jump—up! up!" exhorted Sam, holding a stick a few inches above the ground, while Spang stood looking at it, wagging his tail, but otherwise not making the slightest movement.

" There's been a bit of a bother about a fire at Rookmere—not a very big fire," said Val, simply longing to tell Mrs. Seyton how badly things were going with her, and hoping to find relief in an account of the last misfortune. And she told the tale.

" That's a pity," said Mrs. Seyton, putting an arm round Sammy, who had given up Spangie as a bad job, and, leaving him to worry the stick at will, stood at his mother's knee to listen round-eyed to Val's story. " But I'll speak to Robert Hayling about it. He's connected with my husband's family, you know —we used to see something of him, but I've grown lazy about seeing anyone. I'm nearly a hermit, in fact——"

" You aren't like a hermit at all," broke in Sammy. " Women can't be hermits, because they haven't got beards. And Uncle Bob is cross—I don't like him."

" Oh, *you*," said Mrs. Seyton, giving him a little tweak. " We'll see what can be done, Val. I shouldn't worry too much about it."

" You've got my four-leaved clover, you know," said Sammy, in a rather doubtful voice, as if he wanted to believe it an all-powerful charm, but couldn't make himself do it. " That will bring you luck, and make everything come right, won't it?"

" It's brought one bit of luck already," said Val, stroking Spangie, who, finding himself neglected, had brought up the stick, and stood eagerly waiting to be asked to perform some marvel with it. " It's brought me back here. I feel different all through since I came."

Mrs. Seyton gave her another quick look.

" If that means ' happier ' we must see that you come a very great deal," she said.

CHAPTER XIX

Enter Sammy

Val went to school on Monday morning with an unusual feeling. Generally she was glad when a weekend at The Turret was over, and there was the certainty of spending most of her time at Myra Dakin's, but she now felt that she wouldn't be sorry when the term was ended. And this feeling became much stronger when, after prayers, Miss Beauchamp announced that, owing to a regrettable incident that had occurred the Saturday before last on the Rookmere estate, she wished no picnic excursions to be made by Myra Dakin girls unless they were accompanied by a mistress or some responsible person.

"The Upper Fifth are furious about this," said Pauline. "Some of them had planned a binge, and they say it would lose all its character if they were accompanied by a responsible person. That's a ghastly situation—no one could want to put any unfortunate mistress into it—as if they didn't suffer enough through the week."

" We shan't be popular," sighed Julie. " Not that we care. I'm above popularity, myself."

" I've an idea that Mr. Hayling may come round," said Val. " A relation-in-law of his is speaking to him on the subject."

" Ah, but there's Miss Beauchamp to be dealt with now, too. I don't suppose this relation-in-law will take her on."

" It won't hurt the Upper Fifth. Binges go to their heads," said Julie, and, with this poor salve of con- solation, the four settled down to work as Miss Dym- church charged in and began to shoot out exercise books as if they were missiles.

" Aileen Ellerton—not in? Been eating too many ices? Put her book in her desk, Valentine, and I shall count upon you to explain this lesson to her later."

Knowing that this was not mere rhetoric, Val fol- lowed with strained attention. Not until the geometry period was over did she wonder how it would be possible for her to explain anything to Aileen in the present circumstances of their relationship. Mis- tresses never considered that sort of thing—they never seemed to know.

But it was Aileen who got in an explanation first. She appeared at the lunch interval, delivered her note of excuse to Miss Dymchurch, and, rushing up to the big lawn roller, round and on which the Pauline group discussed life while consuming eleven o'clock

buns, she seized Val by the arm, and, with surprising
energy, drew her to another part of the garden.

"Val! To think how you've been treated! I've been
ill all the week-end; really ill. Don't you see how pale
I am?"

"You *do* look a bit sick," agreed Val.

"Well, it isn't over-eating or anything like that, it's
simply what happened on Saturday," declared Aileen,
with such sincerity that Val couldn't help being impressed. "Can you ever, *ever* forgive me?"

"I don't suppose it was your fault," said Val,
glancing round to assure herself that no one had
heard Aileen's dramatically delivered question. "Calm
down, Aileen. You're not on the stage now, you know."

"I wish I wasn't at all—at least I wish—wish you
were too. No, it wasn't my fault, of course it wasn't—
it was Mrs. Wilby's nonsense. I don't know what sort
of rubbish she must have told Mother. And Mother
made the great mistake of not consulting me before
seeing you—turning you away from our very gates.
How can you ever forgive me?"

"Oh, it's all right as far as you're concerned," said
Val. "Don't let's talk about it."

"But it's *terrible*, Val. I used quite to like Mrs.
Wilby—she was always saying nice things to me—
but, why, she's a *poisonous* person. She's dangerous.
I don't know how *you* can like her, Val."

"Well, I don't, much," said Val.

" But something ought to be *done*. I said so. I said you ought to bring an action for libel——"

" What did your mother say?"

" Nothing much. Aunt Carol told me not to be ridiculous, of *course*."

" That's it. That's what any sensible person would say."

" But, *Val*, it's awful! Are you happy, Val? Do you like living at The Turret?"

" No, I'm not. No, I don't. I just hate it," said Val suddenly.

Aileen stared at her, sympathizing with and yet taken aback by her vehemence. She hadn't spoken her feelings before, and now as at last she relaxed control they seemed to spring out with a sort of fury that was surprising in contrast with her usual quick, contained, half humorous utterance, that astonished even herself.

" Well, you mustn't go on doing it. Listen, Val, one thing. I'll go up and see Mr. Hayling about that fire. I'll tell him exactly how I saw it and how I told you. That'll settle that, anyway."

" Do you think it will?" said Val. It didn't seem to matter to her so much just now, for some reason.

" Well, the Fifth seemed to think so."

Jerking herself back to the realization of school politics, lost for a moment in that sudden violent declaration of her sentiments about The Turret, Val

thought that it might still be a good thing for Aileen
to do.

" Go ahead, then."

" Val! I wish you'd come with me."

" Why?"

" I don't know. I hate going alone. I wish you'd
come, Val. I'd come with you if you were the one to
go—or I'd try to, anyway."

Something in Aileen's tone aroused Val's protective
instinct, brought back the sense of " togetherness "
that the two girls never seemed quite able to forget.

" Right," she said. " I'll come. But let's go at once.
Let's go directly after school. If we don't plunge, it'll
be so much worse."

" Oh, Val, I'm so glad. Val, I never meant it when
I said I hated you. I like you better than anybody I've
ever known outside the family, and tons better than
Aunt Carol in it. When I heard what happened on
Saturday, I was simply beside myself. Really, I was.
You do believe it, don't you, Val?"

" Oh, I believe it all right," said Val, with a comical
little look. " Three-thirty this afternoon, then—and
we'll do the deed."

A few weeks ago, Val might have felt some qualms
of shyness about calling at Rookmere, but now she
cared as little as people do when they feel that, if their
fortunes take a turn, it must be one for the better.
Whatever unpremeditated effect their visit might have

on Mr. Hayling, it could hardly be worse than that of Mrs. Wilby's over-hasty apology. However hostile the owner of Rookmere might be, rough outspoken anger would be preferable to her smooth and constant displeasure. " And it's Aileen's affair, of course," thought Val. " Perhaps that's why I'm not particularly scared." But even if it were Aileen's affair, she guessed that when the moment came, she would be spokeswoman, and she was right.

" I've written it all out," said Aileen, in a low tone, as the girls went up a drive beautifully shaded with the arched boughs of beeches, whose leaves were as cool and green as if they had just unfolded from the bud. " But you might say who we are, and why we've come, Val. I never know how to begin, and a good beginning makes such a difference."

" Right you are. But we won't begin. We'll just rush *in medias res*, like epic poetry," said Val, on whom literature lessons were not wasted.

They followed this plan with such success that the bewildered Mr. Seton Hayling had some difficulty in making out who they were, especially as he had a notion that they were in some way connected with a petition for a flower-show, which he was particularly anxious should not be held in the grounds of Rookmere.

" Vicar's field is the place. Best field in the country. Told him so last year," was his comment on Val's opening—" Oh, Mr. Hayling, we've come about that picnic patch—the one between the oaks and the larches——"

" It *looks* a very nice field," said Val. " But, about that place being spoilt——"

" Ah! that's the point. Vicar's field—nothing to spoil—nothing to pick—nothing to destroy. Grass trampled down a bit —soon picks up in a field. Lawns ruined, ruined for a season."

Val wondered by what stretch of imagination the ground between the oaks and the larches, beautiful as it was, could be called a lawn. If Mr. Hayling saw things like that, no wonder he was distressed by the damage done by the fire. But, though his point of view might be bewildering enough to be a little alarming, the man himself was not the fierce landed proprietor she had imagined, full of devices to prevent and punish trespassing, but a being as human as any of her uncles, who might, in the smallest readjustment of circumstances, become as friendly as they were.

" I know—we're tremendously sorry about it. But we didn't do it—we weren't responsible. Aileen found it out, and we did all we could to prevent further damage. That's just what we've come to tell you."

" Oh, you did all you could? And what did you do it with, against that crowd—a pistol?"

" No, a spade—at least, we began with that. The

camp buckets of water finished it off, but it had gone pretty far——"

The door burst open.

" Please, Uncle Bob, I've come to tell you about that fire. I made a little fire and I forgot to put it out and it must have caught. Mother said I was to come and say I did it and not Val Forrest."

All three stared with astonishment at the small figure standing straight and resolute before the owner of Rookmere. His shirt was very clean, his grey flannel shorts looked as if they were on for the first time, his blue tie was knotted neatly, and his fair hair was brushed till it shone like spun gold, and parted evenly. Never in the course of their acquaintanceship had Val seen Sammy so immaculate. He had got himself up for his confession, which was evidently costing him a great effort.

"*You* forgot to put out a fire!" roared Mr. Hayling, in a voice as different from that in which he had addressed the girls as a sergeant major's is from the family doctor's. "*You* lit a fire on my property, or on anyone else's, and forgot to put it out!"

" Yes," said Sammy in a low voice.

" D'you know, sir, what boys are who light fires and forget to put them out? D'you know what?"

" Very careless," suggested Sammy, in a small whisper.

" Cads, sir. Cads."

"He's only seven, Mr. Hayling," said Val, who saw that the valiant Sam was nearly crying.

"Only! That's where you women make the mistake. 'Only' this and 'only' that. 'Only', 'only', till it's 'only' the gallows. Harden up, girl, harden up."

The mention of the gallows was too much for Sammy, and he burst into loud sobs.

"Do you know this young man?" Mr. Hayling demanded of Val in a great voice.

"Yes, well. I was his governess for a short time," said Val, with much dignity.

"Governess, were you? Then remove him—remove him into the garden and find him some raspberries—remove him into the greenhouse and cut him a bunch of grapes—show him the fish-pool—do whatever you like. Stop him crying, or he'll frighten his mother. And don't go till I've seen you again. No, young woman"— he detained Aileen—"you'll tell me your story before you've gone from my domain."

Val had an idea of how to deal with Sam when he was naughty and lively—subdued by grief he was so much unlike himself that she was doubtful as to what to do for the best. She asked him one question about that Saturday, and discovered that, in the afternoon, he had again escaped from Miss Sturton, and, having looked for Val and her friends in the woods and failed to find them, had made the little fire to console himself.

"There wasn't any water, and I didn't know how to put it out," he said, in a voice still shaken with tears. "I didn't know anything would catch, till I heard you telling Mums about the fire, and then I thought it might have, and I couldn't go to sleep till I'd asked her, and she said I was to come myself and tell Uncle Bob. And I wish I hadn't! I hate him! I'd like to have a sword in my hand so that I might kill him."

"Don't you feel happy now you've got it off your chest, though?" said Val.

"No, I don't. I'd rather have it on my chest ten times worse than have to breathe a word in the same air as Uncle Bob."

"Well, I think you're all wrong. He had to be a bit cross with you, but he isn't cross right through."

"He *is*. He's a swine. When I'm a man I shall come and call on him and tell him so. I shall go right in without ringing and say 'Swine—*swine*—SWINE'. And if I know anything worse to say by then I shall say it."

"Look, Sam, there's a peacock!" Val tactfully changed the conversation. "Let's see if we can find feathers. I'd love to have a fan made of peacock's feathers. Oh, look! He's spreading his tail!"

Sam gave a most unwilling glance in the direction of the peacock, but he could not resist the beauty of the glorious colour as the bird spread his tail feathers, and gazed for a moment enchanted.

" I wonder if that tail's as good all round," he then said. " You keep him occupied in front, Val, and I'll steal quietly to the back and see."

Relieved at his interest, Val obligingly mildly annoyed the peacock, while Sam, with the gesture of a cinema sleuth, crept along the grass. Then he stopped short, straightened himself, and thrust his hands in his pockets, with a look of disgust and triumph.

" Sucks for Uncle Bob!" he said. " It isn't."

CHAPTER XX

A Visit and a Return

Going home, with a basket of big, dark red, bloomy raspberries and a bunch of white roses, Val wondered at the pleasant happenings of the afternoon. " A lot of misfortunes can come in a very short time," she reflected, " and so can a lot of lucky things." It was almost unbelievable that all at once the mystery of the fire had been cleared up, and Mrs. Wilby's apology set aside, while Mr. Hayling had expressed to Aileen and Val the gratitude they no longer expected. " Right of way through Rookmere to you," he said. " To you and your friends—picnic, camp, anything of the sort. Except a flower-show. Can't endure a flower-show, whatever the circumstances."

" Oh, we shan't want a flower-show," Val assured him, her heart glowing with the thought that the dream of the Fifth might be realized, and that they might camp by that perfect lake. But Aileen must come too. Now the part she had played in earning the right of way privilege was acknowledged, the Fifth would be sorry for the mistakes they had made about her, and want to atone for them. Val felt instinctively that, given sufficient evidence, Pauline was the sort of person who is capable of owning herself in the wrong.

Pauline didn't, openly. She said not a word on the subject to Aileen, but asked her to play singles at tennis, and, as Aileen waited with her dripping swimming dress by the mangle at the Baths, stretched out a hand with a " Here, I'll do it after mine ". To wring out anyone else's bathing-dress was a recognized sign of friendship at Myra Dakin's, and Aileen had been there long enough to know it. She had been there long enough to value it, too, and she now saw the Fifth as beings capable of kindliness and fun rather than as " those hateful girls " whose one desire was to torment her.

Mr. Hayling made his mistake quite clear in a letter to Miss Beauchamp, and the Fifth and Sixth were detained after prayers to hear that there was no ban upon unofficial school picnicking, with added remarks on the demeanour of the good picnicker in general, and of Myra Dakin's girls in particular, and a word or two of praise for Aileen and Val's promptitude and success in extinguishing what might have been a dangerous fire. Val wondered if she should report this to Mrs. Wilby, and decided that there would be no point in doing so. " It would only seem as if I were trying to crow because she had made a mistake," she thought.

" That is, if she believed it. Ten to one she wouldn't."
And so, with the reticence that was one of the strangest
qualities in the new Val Forrest, she said not a word
about it.

But of another piece of news she did speak—it
would have been impossible to have kept silent about
it. It was Pauline who gave it, and Val rushed home
for luncheon, eager to have it confirmed, though she
was sure there was no mistake: it was too good not
to be true.

" Mrs. Wilby—Mrs. Wilby—have you had a letter?
Is there one for me? Mother's coming home!"

Mrs. Wilby stared at Val. Her usual serenity was
disturbed: her cheeks flushed a curious pale purple
tinge, and her eyes protruded, as if she had been
badly startled.

" Rubbish, child!" she said sharply. " I heard
from Mr. Hunniker a week or two ago. He did not
mention it."

" But it's true—it's true," sang Val. " She's coming
with Pauline's people, just on a visit, to see me. Mr.
Hunniker wants her to come. I 'spect he's sent her
for the holiday, to recover—he's a generous old bird,
really: his one drawback is that he thinks girls a
nuisance."

" A drawback many people must share with him."
As soon as the words were out of her mouth Val
waited to hear that said. But it wasn't said: in fact,

Mrs. Wilby did not seem to notice that she had spoken. She just stared at her. Suddenly Val was frightened. She had heard of people having fits—perhaps this fixed look was the first symptom. She didn't want Mrs. Wilby to have a fit—she wouldn't know what to do for her.

" I say—do you feel ill?" she asked nervously. " Shall I fetch your smelling salts—or ring for Cooling?"

What ringing for Cooling would achieve she was uncertain, but the suggestion sounded sensible enough.

" No, no. Do no such thing. Your news is so sudden—it seems most peculiar that I should not have heard. Naturally I am upset."

" It's good news, though, isn't it?" said Val, her ardour a little damped, but not quenched.

" Very good indeed. And perhaps you will find out from your friends when we may expect your mother?"

" I expect you'll get a cable or letter," said Val. " Perhaps she wanted to keep it a surprise for me. But Pauline didn't say it was a secret."

" A surprise. Yes, dear. Quite," said Mrs. Wilby, and said no more.

A few days later Aileen came to school in a state of excitement, almost as joyful as Val's had been when she heard her good news from Paul.

" Isn't it gorgeous, Val?"

" Isn't what gorgeous?"

" That you're coming to spend this week with us. Oh, I know it's nothing to *you*, but I shall love it, simply *love* it."

" It's nothing to me because I don't know anything about it," said Val. " Tell me, Aileen. I'm really quite interested."

" Why, Mrs. Wilby's off to Tunbridge Wells, or one of those places with mineral waters," said Aileen. " And she asked Mother if she could put you up " (" put up with " had been the expression, but Aileen tactfully paraphrased it) " for a few days, and Mother was beside herself with relief at the notion, as she's secretly quite sick with shame at having been taken in as she was about you. She told Mrs. Wilby so, too, and Aunt Carol was in at the time, so I expect she also had a few words to say on the subject."

" But—Aileen——"

" Oh, Val, you aren't sorry, are you? You do want to come, don't you? You know you hate being at The Turret: you said so."

" Well, I hope you didn't tell anyone that. I can stand anything now Mother's coming." Val stopped short, her heart sick with dread. " Aileen—you don't think—Mrs. Wilby couldn't be going to Liverpool or Glasgow to meet Mother — to keep her from coming?"

" Val, don't be so silly! As if she could! You're morbid!"

"If you wanted anything to happen as badly as I want Mother to come you might seem morbid about it too," said Val. "And it's so queer—arranging for me to stay with you without saying a word to me about it—don't you think so yourself?"

"But Mrs. Wilby *is* queer where you're concerned," said Aileen. "I shouldn't worry about that. Just forget about her, and let's have a real good time together."

"Perhaps she'll tell me when I go home for luncheon," said Val.

"But you aren't going home for luncheon," said Aileen, with a delighted squeal. "That's the beauty of it—no horrible waiting and thinking that perhaps you won't come after all. You're coming home with me after school—and staying, too."

"But what about my suit-case?" said Val, with a curiously hopeless sensation, as if her life were being taken out of her hands.

"Don't worry about your suit-case. I expect it'll be waiting at Lyncote station when we get there to-night. Aunt Carol's actually sending down the car to meet us."

Everything seemed hopelessly well arranged. She couldn't have believed that she would ever want to go to The Turret, but, could she have slipped away from Aileen and returned to find out from Mrs. Wilby what it all meant, Val would have done so. It was,

however, impossible. With Aileen she took the afternoon train to Lyncote, found her two suit-cases, neatly
strapped and labelled, already stowed in Miss Ellerton's car, and was received, with effusiveness that was
almost tearful, by Mrs. Ellerton. Once at Lyncote
House, her fears, tiresome and uncontrollable as vague
fears are, almost ceased to haunt her. The comfort,
the good food, the kindness of both Aileen's mother
and Aunt Carol, affected her as they were bound to
do: she felt easier and gayer, and the queer reticence
and suspicion that were no part of her nature seemed to
slip away from her. But, one afternoon of an " early
day ", when playing tennis with Aileen before em-
barking on home lessons which they did rather well
in one another's company, she felt with startling
suddenness the presentiment that had troubled her
when she knew she was to leave The Turret for this
visit. She flung down her racket.

" Aileen! It's dreadful to think that I don't know
when Mother's coming! Paul doesn't know when her
people are due to sail."

" But it'll be soon, Val, you know that. They were
only there for that conference."

" Supposing she goes to The Turret and doesn't
find me there! Supposing she can't find me!"

" *Val!* Pauline knows you are here—naturally Mrs.
Forrest would go round to her."

" But Pauline's people don't live here—that aunt

and uncle, I mean. They live up north. Oh, Aileen, if anything comes in the way——"

" Let's get the paper and see when the boats are due to arrive."

" They're arriving every week-end. Why don't I *know*."

" Why not go to The Turret and leave a note on the door?" said Aileen practically.

Val caught at the suggestion with the eagerness for definite action felt by those whose nerves are on edge.

" Now. I'll go *now*," she said.

" But, Val——"

" Oh, let me, Aileen. Let me."

Two months ago Aileen would have pouted and sulked, but her friendship for Val was growing big enough to push out the little childish grievances that had spoiled her. She threw down her racket, but without temper.

" All right. Hurry up. I'll tell Mother you won't be in for tea. No, don't wait—I'll take in the rackets and balls. If you must go, get it over."

" I'm sorry." Aileen's acquiescence made Val feel that she was acting unreasonably. " But I must. I couldn't settle down to homework till I've been."

Aileen nodded. Val felt in her pocket for her unusually fat purse (Mrs. Wilby had put five shillings at the top of one of the suit-cases) rammed her school sailor well down over her rather dishevelled hair, and ran to the station as if she were on some errand involving life and death, rather than gratifying what her reasonable self told her might be only a whim. But she dared not listen to that self, so strongly did her instinct urge her on.

She had only two minutes to wait for a Dakin Priors train, and it was not long before she found herself walking up the familiar road that led to The Turret. Her heart hammered; she ached with apprehension. " What *is* the matter with you? Keep calm!" she said to herself, but still the uncomfortable excitement persisted. Her hand trembled so much that she could hardly open the hated gate of the dreary little front garden. Then, quieted by astonishment, she stood still.

The Turret was not, as she had expected, shut up, with blinds drawn and brasses unpolished. The windows were wide open. There was a bowl of marigolds on the table of the room Mrs. Wilby had called her " snuggery ". A half eaten green apple and a rag doll of disreputable appearance lay on the grass by the garden seat, and, on the second step of the short flight leading to the " Salve " mat, a tabby kitten was stretched motionless, as if it had unintentionally toppled over asleep in the midst of play. Val looked again at the name on the gate. She had made no mistake. This was The Turret.

Carefully avoiding the kitten, she walked up to the

door and pressed the bell. A slightly tousled, but pleasant-looking maid answered the ring. A baby of about two years old tottered after her, and stood sucking his thumb and gazing at Val as she asked for Mrs. Wilby.

" Mrs. Wilby? Oh, she's gone away. She was the last tenant. It's Mrs. Hollyoake now."

" Gone away—for good?"

" I don't know, Miss. She may come back to Dakin Priors, or she may be there now. I should inquire at the Post Office if I was you. The house was shut for a few days and we haven't been redirecting letters. Did you want her particularly, Miss?" seeing the surprise and concern on Val's face.

" Well—I didn't think she had gone. If a Mrs. Forrest comes here will you tell her that Val Forrest is staying with the Ellertons at Lyncote House, Lyncote?"

" I'll tell her. And I'll tell the mistress when she comes in," said the girl good-naturedly.

" Oh, thanks, if you would. I'll write it down." Val found a pencil in her pocket, and the maid found an advertisement of cocoa behind the door, and on the shiny smooth paper the address was duly recorded.

" I'll be sure to tell her," promised the maid again, as Val turned to go.

" So long, old sing," remarked the baby unexpectedly.

Val laughed and waved to him, but she was hardly conscious of his charms. As she shut the gate she would probably never open again, her mind was in a tumult. What was happening to her? Why had Mrs. Wilby left The Turret like this? Would the Ellertons know? What did it all mean?

Then, as she turned down the station road, she saw someone coming, lightly built and quick of step as she herself; dark, too, and grey·eyed, but with a look that was steady though troubled—the look of the grown-up woman, not of Viola wrecked on her island. Val stopped short for a minute—she didn't know that travelling-coat—then, with a funny little squeak, she sprang forward.

"Mother, Mother—I *knew* there was something— oh, Mother!"

CHAPTER XXI

Round the Camp-fire

It was twilight, September twilight, mellow, with the promise of stars. Val turned into the Rookmere plantation of larches and firs to fill her pockets with cones. The Fifth Formers at the camp might think it a waste of carrying power, but she couldn't pass cones: to see them melt from their hard carved-looking woodenness to little red flowers of flame, with a burning fragrance sweeter than incense, was a pleasure to be gratified whenever possible. They were light, too. When she had stuffed the pockets of her blazer and skirt as full as she could, she pressed a few small ones among the parcels of her rücksack, and, slinging it over her shoulders and adjusting the straps, took the grassy drive towards the mere just as Arcturus was showing faintly in the west.

No one can walk at a good round pace through a wood. Val did not loiter, as she would have done in the sun and shadow of the afternoon, but she went softly, her mind thronged with thoughts of her first term in the Fifth at Myra Dakin's, with her experiences at The Turret, that now seemed so far away that they might have been a tale she had read or heard someone tell, of the rapidity with which, after her mother's coming, events had adjusted and readjusted themselves, leaving her safe and happy in a new life. " Established at the court of Illyria," she thought, remembering, with a little smile, the fall of the curtain at the end of the second afternoon performance of *Twelfth Night*, in which, at the urgent plea of Aileen, she had been reinstated, and played her never-forgotten part of Viola. And the court of Illyria in this case must have been Thornytangle, where her mother had left her under the pleased charge of Mrs. Seyton, when, two days ago, she had sailed to Montreal after her six weeks in England. The Hunnikers wanted her back, and, this time, she went with a sense of peace, having seen for herself where Val was, and left her among good friends.

It was curious, thought Val, walking through the wood, the suddenness with which events came about. One day your whole life seemed to be set and fixed in a certain way, dominated by some happy or unhappy fact: next it was all different. Did things always change like this? Pauline said there was a kind that didn't. " Take my young brother Thomas." said Pauline. " He turned from a baby like Angela into himself, and nobody noticed it." But the events of Val's life had certainly up till now shifted and readjusted themselves with speed. One day her mother and herself had been quite well off; the next came the news of the failure of Marraby's and they were poor. One day they had thought they would live together till Val was a woman; the next came Cousin John Hunniker's letter and separation. One day it had seemed that Mrs. Wilby, with her curious faculty of pinching up life and making it cramped and unhappy, would dominate Val's schooldays; the next she had disappeared—gone as completely as an uneasy dream or the cruel stepmother of the fairy tales. Val couldn't believe this; she almost regretted it. She recalled how she and her mother had talked it all over.

" You know, darling," she said to her mother. " I should just love you to have seen her. I'd like to know what you thought of her. I wonder if she'd put that hand on you and give you a warm kiss, and you'd feel pins and needles prickling all over you."

" She might, but we should have quite a lot to talk about first," said Mrs. Forrest. " The question of your pocket-money, for instance, and the incidental expenses at Myra Dakin's. I'm not much of a business woman, but I'd show a firm grip of that situation. I only hope I'll have the chance to do it yet."

Val looked thoughtful. It seemed so strange to think that she hadn't in any way been dependent on Mrs. Wilby; that an ample, even generous sum had been paid for her board and lodging expenses, and allowed for her pocket-money. This was the first time she had come across unfair and mean dealing, and it puzzled her.

" I didn't know misers could be like Mrs. Wilby, quite nice-looking and youngish and living in an ordinary way," she said. " I thought they were all like Silas Marner or old Scrooge. You'd never know —people like the Ellertons would never guess."

" Some people guessed, though," said Mrs. Forrest, with a little smile. " Betty Seyton knew there was something wrong somewhere, and as for that character Ashdown——"

" Ashdown's a sleuth, of course," said Val. " She ought to change her profession. She'd be far more of a help than ' my dear Watson ', any day."

" I must say that those anonymous communications *did* help to bring me home—to see what sort of arrangement I'd been rushed into making for you. It *should* have been all right—Flora Wilby, Flora Hicks we called her then, seemed a harmless enough person in the old days. We quarrelled once or twice—but there's nothing in quarrelling once or twice, generally —it seemed so much better to leave you with some one I knew a little than with a complete stranger. I didn't know enough, of course, not nearly enough."

" Mrs. Seyton says she was a bit malicious at school," ventured Val. " She says she was jealous of you, for one thing."

" Jealous? Oh, rubbish! She couldn't have been—

no material," said Val's mother. "We liked one another all right, as far as I can remember."

"She didn't like *me*, anyway," said Val. "I've never been not-liked like that before. It's different squabbling with someone and just keeping away—it was different even when Aileen used to go off the deep end. This was so—so—ungettable, somehow, and it was always worrying you to get at it."

"Well, never mind about that, now. It's over and ended, and perhaps you'll never come across another Mrs. Wilby. These things always teach you to know your way about in human nature, anyhow."

"That's what Pauline says," agreed Val. "Pauline says I ought to be thankful for coming across such a perfect specimen of—of—I don't know what she called it. Pauline has invented Latin names for people, like specimens——"

"'Pauline says!'" Mrs. Forrest laughed. "How you girls do talk! But I suppose you've got to go through with being yourselves."

"But Paul's a nice self, isn't she, Mother? She isn't priggish, you know, not an atom. She's just got an ear for the savage breast, instead of having an ear for music."

"An ear for——? My darling, it sounds a dreadful misfortune. Anyway, we'll have Paul for a week-end, frivolous if possible, when I've made a plan or two about where to spend my short time here."

Some of that short time had been spent with the Ellertons, who loved having visitors, and it was during her stay there that Val's mother received a letter from Mrs. Wilby, written from a hotel in Southampton. She was going abroad for a little, she said, and words could not express her disappointment at being unable to meet her old friend Rose Faukner. The visit to Tunbridge Wells, which was to have been just a tiny one, had resulted in her meeting with certain other very very dear old friends, and so had extended itself. They had planned a year's travel together. It was a great disappointment to be unable to offer a home, a simple little home, but still a *home* to dear Valentine, and she only hoped that no difficulty would be experienced in making other arrangements for her.

" *Well!*" was all the comment made by Mrs. Forrest on reading this epistle, which she passed to Miss Ellerton.

" Doesn't explain why she evidently didn't mean to return to The Turret when she left Dakin Priors for a few days," said that lady. " Doesn't explain much at all unless you read between the lines."

" If Cousin John Hunniker knew all about this he'd never again trust me to make a money arrangement," said Mrs. Forrest. " Still, still, I hope to meet Mrs. Wilby."

" Give it up," snapped Miss Ellerton. " You won't."

And she was right. Mrs. Wilby did not again visit

Dakin Priors. As Val said, quoting, she had always disliked unpleasantness. She had gone for good. And, thought Val (walking through the wood), not to see herself as Mrs. Wilby saw her, was like coming out of a room of distorting mirrors and being just ordinary Val Forrest again, as once, in a sort of panic, she had felt she never could be.

Val Forrest, with the next few years before her like a pleasant journey. A remove into the Upper Fifth; a year in the Sixth as a prefect. Friendships, games, Shakespeare lessons, all the interest and endeavour of school. Then Montreal—Mr. Hunniker had liked the way she had written about her mother, wanted to see her. Montreal, the house with the great porch flanked with tubs of hydrangeas, and the grassy lawn running, without boundary hedge, straight on to the public way. Riding on Mount Royal, skating and sledging in winter. The university, perhaps. Val liked the notion of it. Her mother had pleased her with the description of the wide fair city, like a French city, like an English one, like a Canadian one, like itself. She didn't want to leave Myra Dakin's and England just now. But when the time came she would be ready.

" Val! Val!"

" Coo-oo—"

Cries from the little group round the burning logs by the lake. Val flung off her rücksack, emptied her pockets of cones, and sat on the grass by Pauline, who, thin dark face sharp against the flames, hair wreathed with a trail of red berries, looked like a witch intent on some charm worked in the shifting, darting light of the camp-fire.

" Where's Mrs. Seyton?"

" Not come up yet."

Mrs. Seyton, warden of the camp, tramped up from Thornytangle every night to sleep, with Sammy, in a small green tent which she said had been pitched on all the best secret camping sites of the British Isles. " In the days before I grew lazy, Val." Sammy presumably was asleep in its shelter now. Val made no inquiry about him, fearing lest the mere mention of his name should make him spring from his bracken mattress and refuse to return to it again.

" It's decent of her to fag up here every night. Not that we shouldn't be quite safe by ourselves. Of course we should."

" She brings up topping things to eat," said Julie with appreciation. " And doesn't dwell on failures— that hen, for instance. Tell Val about the hen, Paul."

" Well, we were feeling a bit above ourselves, so Julie ordered a young fowl from Derwent's farm and got it at one and six—a bargain. It seemed cheap, but they swore it would boil——"

" It was terribly long in the leg," said Aileen. " We had to fold it up to put it in the pot."

" And it was so *emaciated*," said Paul thoughtfully.
" We thought stuffing might help it to swell up a bit,
but we hadn't the material to make it, so we put an
egg-cup in it to make it stick up nicely, just as you do
in a fruit tart."

" But it was no good. It just draped itself round
the egg-cup, and, in the boiling, it simply faded away.
It was really a phenomenon. We cooked it quite
slowly, too, just one bubble——"

" Like a puncture," sighed Julie.

" And Mrs. Seyton came along for luncheon, and
tackled a wing bone. We'd have given her a slice of
breast, but there was nothing you could carve, you
could only dissect. And she didn't gibe: she only said
how good it smelt."

" All she could say, and she said it."

" And two days afterwards she sent Ashdown—it
was before Ashdown went to Margate—along with a
perfectly glorious cold chicken, with salad and bread-
sauce."

" *Enough* bread sauce. It's the only time in my life
I've ever had quite enough," said Julie in a tone of
reminiscent solemn joy.

" Mrs. Seyton is the sort of person who gives
people enough," said Paul. " Of all kinds of things,
not only bread sauce."

" Sammy, for instance," said Julie.

" S-s-sh! Don't breathe his name," implored four

hushed voices, and the girls looked anxiously towards the green tent. But all was silence: evidently Sam slumbered peacefully.

" I'm glad I'm going to live with her," said Val, clasping her hands round her knees and rocking herself in the firelight. " And I'm glad we're having a whole fortnight here before school, and I'm glad I know Paul, and Aileen, and Corinna, and Julie, and I'm glad I'm at Myra Dakin's——"

" In fact, you're glad to be Val Forrest," said Paul, discovering Val's hoard of cones and throwing them on to the fire.

" Well—just now, I believe I am," said Val. And, as the fire found the cones, and leapt and gleamed and danced up into the darkness, she gave a little laugh, just because she was so happy.